• • • • • •

Asha's eyes were wide and frozen in place. "Wha, who's Mr. Brown?"

"Prolly the biggest boss in the city," Boom informed her. "He got hundreds of niggas working under him. He into everything from gun running to prostitutes and dope. If it was anybody else, I would step in and try to cool this shit down. But Mr. Brown is on a whole 'nother level. That nigga like John Gotti. Don't nobody fuck with that man. Yo cousin stupid for getting involved with anybody that got something to do with him."

Asha's mouth went dry. Next to her sister, Tristan was her closest relative.

"Wha–" She cleared her throat. "What can we do about it?"

"Tell him to pay what he owe," Boom advised her. "That's it." His eyes were stern when he said, "Don't get involved with this shit, Asha. Don't get nowhere near it. I know since you been down with this murder game, you think a bullet can solve any problem. But Mr. Brown ain't the one to fuck with. He got too many killers on his payroll. He the most dangerous man I know."

Asha was really spooked now. She thought Boom was the most dangerous man in the world. To hear him speak of another man with that level of reverence spoke volumes.

"Okay," she said. "I won't get involved. I'll talk to my cousin, tell him to pay what he owe."

"If you gotta give him that money," he said, referring to the five thousand he just gave her, "do it. It's better to pay his debt than go to his funeral."

Asha nodded. Her heart was racing. "Okay, Boom. Thanks for letting me know."

He gave her another hard look before pushing off the bed. He hefted the duffle bag and headed for the door. "A'ight. I'm out. I'll holler at you later."

• • • • • •

ASHA AND BOOM PART 2

KEITH THOMAS WALKER

KEITHWALKERBOOKS, INC

KEITHWALKERBOOKS

Publishing Company
KeithWalkerBooks, Inc.
P.O. Box 690
Allen, TX 75013

For information write
KeithWalkerBooks, Inc.
P.O. Box 690
Allen, TX 75013

ISBN-13 DIGIT: 978-1-7356151-0-3
ISBN-10 DIGIT: 1-7356151-0-2
Library of Congress Control Number: 2020918987
Manufactured in the United States of America

Second Edition

Visit us at www.keiththomaswalker.com

This book is for Dorel Anderson

CONTENTS

MORE BOOKS BY KEITH THOMAS WALKER

Blurred Lines: The Monster
Blurred Lines: Cop Killer
Blurred Lines: Copycat Killer
Blurred Lines: Mister Me Too

Asha and Boom Part 1
Asha and Boom Part 2
Asha and Boom Part 3

Backslide
Backslide 2

The Realest Ever
The Realest Christmas Ever

Prom Night at Finley High
Fast Girls at Finley High
Bullies at Finley High

Jackson Memorial
Jackson Memorial 2

Brick House
Brick House 2
Brick House 3

Threesome
Threesome 2

Take One of Mine
Take one of Mine Part 2

Fixin' Tyrone
How to Kill Your Husband
A Good Dude
Riding the Corporate Ladder
The Finley Sisters' Oath of Romance
Blow by Blow
Jewell and the Dapper Dan
Harlot
Plan C (And More KWB Shorts)
Dripping Chocolate
Sleeping With the Strangler
Life After
Blood for Isaiah
One on One
Election Day
Evan's Heart
Poor Righteous Poet
Might be Bi Part One
Harder
Primal Part One
Hotline Fling

Visit www.keiththomaswalker.com for information about
these and upcoming titles from KeithWalkerBooks

PROLOGUE
BRIONNA

CHAPTER
1

AT ELEVEN P.M., was moderately populated, which was typical for a weeknight. On the weekends, the club manager drew large crowds with popular artists like DaBaby and Meek Mill. But on Wednesdays, the DJ spun old school classics, while a line dance instructor taught couples synchronized dance moves that seemed complicated from Mike's perspective. But he observed a few newbies who seemed to be catching on fairly quickly, so maybe the dances weren't as hard as they appeared.

Mike sat alone at a table near the bar, nursing a Cognac and Coke that he couldn't manage to get to the bottom of. Every time his busty waitress noticed he was a few sips shy of having only ice in his glass, she approached the table and replaced it with a fresh drink. Mike wondered why she assumed he'd want more to drink, rather than ask. She wasn't wrong, but he didn't appreciate her being so presumptuous.

Mike's lifestyle generally allowed and oftentimes required him to turn up, but tonight he preferred the relatively quiet atmosphere. He watched the line dancers, the bartender and the waitresses go about their routine. There were more women in the club than men, some of whom were taking turns dancing with a well-dressed old head who knew all the moves. But Mike didn't approach any of the single ladies and ask if they wanted to show him how to line dance.

He wasn't looking for companionship, but he also wasn't blind. He couldn't help but notice a light-skinned cutie who entered the club alone. She walked through the dimly lit establishment with an air of familiarity, first checking out the buffet and then the dance floor before finding an empty table a few spots away from his. She took a seat and scanned the club again. She noticed Mike and saw that he noticed her too. He offered a smile. She returned it before digging her phone from her purse and giving the device her attention.

The newcomer wasn't glamourous or scantily clad, but she held Mike's attention for the next five minutes. Her hair was braided up top before falling into lose curls around her shoulders. Her makeup was moderate. She was more skinny than fine, but Mike thought she had a nice figure. She wore a black tube dress that hugged her frame, accentuating her breasts, hips and slim waistline. Her skin was so fair, she might have been mixed, but Mike couldn't detect any culture in her features other than black. He watched as a waitress came and took her drink order. When she delivered the beverage, Mike left his table and stepped to the beauty.

"You here alone?"

She looked up at him. Mike wore a long-sleeved, white button down with blue khakis. His hair was shaved low, his face clean shaven. His skin was dark, his physique slim. He could tell by the look in her eyes that she liked what she saw.

She nodded. "Yeah. I'm here by myself."

"Mind if I join you?"

He waited for her to shrug before he pulled out the chair across from her and sat down. She continued perusing her phone for a few moments before placing it on the table and looking him in the eyes.

"You been here before?" he asked. "You like this place?"

"I been here a couple of times," she replied, watching him intently. "I don't like the buffet, but I usually like the music."

"You line dance?" he asked, looking back at the dance floor.

She shook her head. "I didn't know that's what they had going on tonight. You dance?"

"No, not like that."

"You didn't know tonight was line dancing either?"

"Yeah, I knew," Mike replied.

"So you like watching people dance, even though you're not into it?" She smiled at him.

He smiled back. "They look like they're having fun, but I'm not good at memorizing dance moves. I can't even do the Cupid Shuffle. What you drinking?"

"D'Usse."

"You drinking it straight?" He checked her glass. "On the rocks?"

She nodded.

"You got good taste. Most people – *most women* – get it with Coke, messing up the flavor."

"Most women can't handle a straight drink," she replied. "After two or three, they liable to leave the club with *whoever*."

He chuckled and then asked, "Want me to get you another?"

She looked down at her full glass and chuckled. "After what I just said, you trying to get me liquored up?"

"No. I'm trying to be a gentleman. You made it sound like you can handle it."

"I can," she said and quickly downed her drink as he watched. "I guess I'll take another."

Mike waved the waitress over without taking his eyes off her. One of his eyebrows was raised, as was the corner of his mouth. He ordered both of them another round.

When the waitress walked away, his new friend asked, "What's your name?"

"Banks."

She grinned. "That's your real name?"

He shook his head. "Naw, that's what people call me."

"Why they call you that? Wait, let me guess, you a baller, right?"

He smiled. His teeth were nice and straight. "I guess I'm something like that."

"What kind of baller?" she wondered. "You don't dress like a dealer, and you're not big enough to play sports."

"That's offensive."

"I guess you could play basketball," she conceded, "but you not tall enough for that."

"And the insults keep coming..."

She laughed. Mike thought she had pretty lips. She struck him as a little hood, but he thought she had a sophistication about her.

"What about you," he asked. "What's your name?"

"B.B."

He frowned. "I *never* would've guessed that. It don't fit you at all."

"Why you say that?"

"B.B. sounds like somebody's country-ass auntie."

She laughed again. "It's better than running around bragging about how much money you got – or fronting about money you don't got."

"Oh, don't worry. I wouldn't let nobody call me Banks if it wasn't true."

She rolled her eyes. "Don't matter to me. I ain't trying to get in your pockets."

They quieted while the waitress delivered their drinks.

When she was gone, Mike asked, "What does B.B. stand for?"

She told him, "The first B's for Brionna."

"*Brionna*? Damn. That's a nice name. Why you let people call you B.B., when they could call you by your real name?"

She shrugged. "The streets gave me that name. Usually when the streets give you a name, you gotta go by it, even if you don't like it."

"*The streets*? What a pretty, young thang like you know about the streets?"

"Prolly a lot more than you."

"Oh, is that right?"

She nodded. "Yeah, I'm pretty sure."

"I doubt that very seriously."

After a pause, she said, "You didn't ask me what the other B is for..."

"That's 'cause I like *Brionna*. I can't see myself calling you B.B."

"But the other B is important," she said. "They go together. Can't have Brionna without the other B."

He frowned curiously. "I can tell you're itching to tell me, so go ahead. What does the other B stand for?"

With a straight face, she told him, "Boom."

The color drained from his face. "Wh, what was that?"

She repeated the name. "Boom."

His mouth went dry, but he managed to ask, "*Brionna Boom*?"

She nodded. She saw his fingers tremble around his glass.

"You're *Brionna Boom*?"

She nodded again, her features expressionless.

His chest heaved. "Wh, what..." He looked around anxiously. "You Boom's girl?"

She didn't respond.

He looked around more frantically. "What are you..." He swallowed roughly. "You come here for me?"

"Yes, I'm here for you, Mike."

He brought a hand to his mouth. His eyes were as big as doorknobs. His mouth stretched into a wretched frown. "This, this got something to do with Tank? I'm – I'm gon' pay that man"

"You got all the answers," Asha said. "Only thing left to figure out is where's the money?"

"*I got it*," he cried. "I told him I was gon' pay him. He didn't have to send you after me. I told him I had his money."

"Where it's at tho?"

"Please," he said, rising from his seat. "Please don't do this. I'ma, I'ma pay that man. I swear," he nearly shrieked. He hastily dug a stack of money from his pocket. He tossed a hundred-dollar bill on the table for their drinks.

Asha didn't rise from her seat, but she asked him, "Where you going, Mike?"

"I'ma, I'ma go get the money. I can – I can bring it to you or give it to him. How he, how he want this to go? I got it. I swear."

Asha was still casual as she asked, "Want me to go with you to get it?"

"Please don't do this," he said, nearly in tears. "Tell Tank I'ma pay him. You ain't gotta do me like this."

Asha shook her head in disappointment.

Mike looked like he pissed his pants.

"God, please don't do me like this," he whimpered as he backed away from the table. When she didn't get up to follow him, he turned and headed for the exit. He looked back at Asha a few times before disappearing out of sight. She was still watching him, but she didn't make any moves in his direction.

CHAPTER
2

ASHA EXITED THE club a minute later and headed for the SUV she arrived in. When she got there, she saw her man loading a lifeless man into the backseat. Boom wore all black, his beard in full flair, his ball cap further obscuring his identity.

He told her, "Get the zip ties."

Asha retrieved them and helped bind Mike's hands behind his back, once Boom got him in the truck. They exited the parking lot thirty seconds later. Boom did not speed once they got on the main thoroughfare.

Asha looked over at him, studying his dark features in the scant lighting.

She asked, "Did he get any licks in on you?"

Boom frowned at that. "Ain't like it was a fight. That nigga damn near ran right up on me. I popped him in the jaw, and he went night night."

Asha chuckled. "I hope you didn't kill him."

Given his size compared to his opponent, Boom couldn't rule that out. They quieted and listened for signs of life from the back seat. Finally they heard the man snoring lightly.

"He'll live, for now," Boom said matter-of-factly.

CHAPTER 3

MIKE AWAKENED IN a brightly lit room with a sharp pain between his ears that was like no headache he'd ever known. As his eyes fluttered open, gaining focus felt like mission impossible, but gradually he became aware of his surroundings. The room appeared to be a small warehouse with sparse furnishings. The smell of dust and mildew was prominent. Mike found he was sitting upright in a chair and he couldn't move his arms. After a brief struggle that sent a biting pain through his wrists, he realized they were bound behind him.

He was not alone in the room. Initially the two figures standing before him were nothing more than a dark blur. Gradually he could make out their features. What he saw stunned the rest of the fog from his mind. Brionna Boom wore the same outfit he'd seen her in earlier. She was just as striking, but now that he knew who she was, he would describe her as *deadly*, rather than beautiful. The man who had given her the last name stood beside her.

Compared to his woman's slim frame, Boom was a hulking beast. His barrel chest protruded though his tee shirt. The muscles in his biceps were intimidating, as he stood with his arms folded under his chest. But nothing was more ominous than the look in his eyes. Mike was acutely aware that few people who had ever seen these killers, individually or as a couple, lived to tell the tale. Droplets of sweat blossomed on his forehead and began to roll down his face. He couldn't stop his eyes from tearing up.

"What happened?" His speech was slurred as his brain struggled to catch up to his thought process. "What happened to my head?"

His jaw was swollen so badly, half of his face looked like a chipmunk storing nuts. Neither Asha nor Boom replied to him.

"*Please don't do this,*" Mike begged. "I can't believe Tank sent y'all after me. It was Tank, right? He the one who did this?"

Boom watched him squirm before responding. "You did this to yourself, Mike." His voice was like a woofer, booming around the empty space. "We never would've snatched you, if you didn't try to get over on that man."

"*I got the money!*" Mike cried. "I told him I had it. He didn't have to do this. All he had to do was call me."

"I ain't got nothing to do with all that," Boom said. "Whatever breakdown in communication you and Tank had, it's too late to go back and fix that."

"*So, you, y'all gon' kill me?*" Mike grimaced, as if the fatal shot was coming at any moment.

Boom shook his head. He told him, "A dead man can't pay his debts. Tank want his money."

"*I got it! I swear I got it!*"

"Where it's at?"

"*I can take you,*" Mike promised. "*We can go right now.*"

Boom nodded. "Bet. That's what I wanted to hear. And don't try nothing slick," he said as he stepped to the man and hoisted him to a standing position. "You know collecting debts ain't what I usually do. I got no problem with bodying you and telling Tank you wouldn't pay."

"*I'ma pay, Boom! I swear!*"

"Man, I ain't trying to hear that shit," Boom replied as he led him to the exit with a firm grip on his arm. "All I need is an address."

CHAPTER
4

MIKE DIRECTED THEM to a home on the north side of town. During the ride, he sat up in the backseat and had regained most of his composure. Possibly sensing his imminent demise, he tried to bargain with the devil.

"Mr. Boom, can't we work out some kind of deal?"

Boom was fairly sure he wouldn't be interested in anything the man had to offer, but he asked him, "What the hell you talking about?"

"I owe Tank two mil'," Mike said, leaning forward in the seat. "How about I give you half a mil', and we can forget this night ever happened? I'll leave the state – or maybe even the country – and you can tell Tank you couldn't find me."

Boom watched his hopeful eyes in the rearview mirror but did not respond. He could smell the desperation wafting from their captive.

"*A whole mil'*," Mike spat. "I'll give you *a million dollars*. I don't know what Tank is paying you for this, but I know it ain't a million dollars. You and your woman can take off, go enjoy life. Tank won't never know about any of this..."

Asha tried not to get too caught up in the particulars of why she and Boom did any job, but at that moment she knew Tank had ample reason to hire them. Even at this late stage of the game, Mike was still conniving; trying to screw his partner yet again.

Asha also wondered if Boom was interested in the offer. From her perspective, it didn't sound like a bad deal. But she couldn't confer with her man at the moment, and Boom's response to Mike was noncommittal.

He simply told him, "Let's see the money first," and continued towards their destination.

CHAPTER 5

TWENTY MINUTES LATER, they pulled up to a three bedroom flat in a neighborhood that didn't look like it had ever seen a hundred thousand, let alone two million dollars at one time. All of the houses on the block, on both sides of the street, weren't worth that much combined.

But Mike told them, "This is it. Pull up in the driveway."

When Boom parked, he turned and asked him, "Is anybody in this house?"

Mike shook his head. "No. This ain't where I live. I come here to hide sometimes, and I keep my money here."

"You got cameras to protect your money when you ain't around?" Boom wanted to know.

"No, but I got a security system, ADT. I would get a notification if somebody ever broke in."

"Not if they know how to disarm it."

"Thing about that is," Mike said, "nobody knows the money's here. Even Tank don't know. If he did, he never would've hired you. Plus, it's not like I got it sitting on the coffee table. Nobody who broke in would ever find it."

"Alright," Boom said. "But if we go in there, and this is some kind of trap, if I see *one* camera, or even if a goddamn chihuahua run up and bite me on the ankle, you a dead man for sure. And it ain't gon' be quick and easy. I'ma make sure you suffer like you ain't never suffered before."

"It ain't no trap, Boom. It's two million in there, and you about to walk out with half of it."

Boom looked Asha's way but didn't let on what he was thinking. He opened his door and casually exited the vehicle.

"Alright, let's go."

CHAPTER 6

INSIDE THE HOUSE, everything Mike had said about the location turned out to be true. There were no cameras, no people and no dogs. He gave Boom the code to disable the alarm and apparently didn't try to trick him with a panic code that would send the police racing to the location.

In the master bedroom, Mike instructed Boom to push the bed all the way to the corner of the room. When Boom did so, neither he nor Asha saw anything amiss with the hardwood floor. Mike directed them to a screwdriver in the nightstand. He told Boom where to insert it and pry up a portion of the floor, revealing a hidden compartment. Asha's eyes widened when she saw two 50-inch duffle bags inside the hole. She couldn't stop her mouth from watering.

Boom told her to check them. Asha unzipped the first bag and saw a pile of neatly stacked greenbacks. Most of the visible currency had Benjamin Franklin's mug on it, with rubber bands around an untold number of smaller stacks. The second duffle bag had identical contents. Asha's heart thundered. This seemed like the score of a lifetime.

"I told you," Mike said, looking down at his loot. "I told you I wasn't playing no–"

Asha didn't see her man produce, point or shoot his weapon, but she heard the muffled *SHUMP* of the silencer. Mike fell face first next to the hole in the floor. Asha was no stranger to murder, but she was caught off guard with this one and couldn't help but flinch as the body impacted the floor with a loud *SMACK*!

Boom took a step forward and put another hole in his head. His expression was as relaxed as it was during the drive to the house. He returned the smoking pistol to the small of his back and pulled a pair of gloves from his pocket. He put them on and then bent and rolled the dead man over. Asha cringed at the destruction the exit wounds had done to his face. She and Boom rarely saw their victims this up close and personal. Even a hardened soldier would react to the sight of exposed brain matter and fresh blood leaking from the wounds.

"Gimme one of them stacks," Boom said.

Asha dutifully reached into one of the bags and grabbed what felt like ten thousand dollars. She handed it to him. Boom pried the dead man's mouth open and stuffed the bills between his teeth. He then pulled his burner phone from his pocket and took a picture of the corpse. One of Mike's eyes was still in good condition. It seemed to be staring right at Asha. She couldn't wait to get out of there.

Three minutes later, they had the money loaded in the SUV. Boom returned to the residence to wipe down all of the surfaces he had touched and of course to set fire to the place. Before meeting him, Asha had only seen one structure fully ablaze. Nowadays, it seemed like a monthly occurrence.

Boom did not speed away from the house. Asha knew this was because the squealing tires might alert a neighbor who may otherwise not notice the fire. Considering the time of night, it was possible the whole house would be destroyed before the first fire truck arrived.

When they got on the freeway, she finally asked him, "Is there any chance we can keep all this money and tell Tank we couldn't find him?"

Boom shook his head.

Their relationship had progressed to the point where she felt comfortable asking, "Why not?"

"Because our reputation means more than this money," he replied. "It's the same reason I didn't take the mil' he was offering and let him go. If he ever told anyone about it, our word would never mean nothing. And the way we left that house, Tank would know no one else could pull that off except for us."

Asha wasn't satisfied. "Yeah, but with two million, we could retire. It wouldn't matter what people think."

Boom did not take offense to her questions. "Maybe we can retire with *five* million, but not two. At the rate we're going, we'll have that in five years. I know it ain't nothing legit about what we do, but I'd rather get paid this way than fuck over our customers."

Asha accepted that, but it also meant she was accepting at least five more years of murder. Even if they did use a sniper rifle most of the time, the deceased all looked like Mike after a run in with Boom and Brionna.

She sighed and settled back in her seat. "How much did this job pay anyway?"

"A lot more than usual," Boom said with a grin. "Retrieving money ain't usually what we do, but the way it pays, I wouldn't turn down another job like this."

A vision of Mike's demolished face suddenly flashed in Asha's mind. The image was so vivid, she felt like she could reach out and touch the blood. She shuddered inwardly and pushed the thought from her consciousness, as she'd learned to do many times in the past.

She looked over at her man and nodded. "Yeah, I wouldn't mind doing another job like this either. It's light work."

Boom smiled. "Oh, I forgot to ask, what you say to Mike to get him to run up out that club like that?"

Asha smiled too. "I told him I was Brionna Boom."

Boom's smile grew wider. "I thought you didn't like that name."

She shrugged. "It's starting to grow on me."

PART ONE
MR. BROWN

CHAPTER
7

BRRRRRRRR
BRRRRRRR
BRRRRRRRRRRR
Asha watched with delight as Boom fed stacks of bills into his money counter and the device whizzed through them, producing a total on the digital screen. So far, the count from their latest customer was dead on. Boom reapplied a rubber band on each $10,000 stack.
BRRRRRRRR
BRRRRRRRRRR
When he was done, he put ten stacks in a duffle bag that was much smaller than the million-dollar bags they pilfered last night, but their haul was still impressive. Boom went to the restroom to wash his hands, because he considered money dirty – not just because of how they obtained it, but because of all the filthy things people do with greenbacks, like hide it in their underwear or shoes.
Asha didn't care how dirty the money was. The moment her man was gone, she slipped out of bed and took

two of the larger stacks from the bag. She knew these had a full range of denominations, which would make it more fun. She returned to the bed and pulled off one of the rubber bands and began to count it. Boom emerged from the restroom and found her lying on her stomach flipping through the bills.

Asha wore only a bra and panties. He admired her figure for a moment before saying, "You don't trust the counter?"

Asha looked over at him, her smile devilish. Boom wore jeans with a white tee and white sneakers. He was cleanshaven this afternoon and without his ball cap – a clear indication that he didn't plan on killing anyone – at least not in the immediate future.

"I trust it," she told him, her eyes back on the money. "I just wanted to count it again. I like money." Her smile widened. "I love the way it feels and smells."

"It's dirty," Boom said. He sat on the bed next to her and palmed one of her butt cheeks. He squeezed it with his large hand.

"I don't care if it's dirty," she replied. "How much do we get to keep after the wash?"

"Tomas takes fifteen percent," Boom said, his eyes on her ass. He used both hands to peel her panties down to her thighs. He massaged her cheeks with both hands and then bent to untie his shoes.

Asha knew Tomas was Boom's most trusted money launderer. The Cuban owned six carwashes, a flower shop and a bakery. Considered one of Overbrook Meadow's most successful self-made entrepreneurs, few knew he took in money from criminals like Boom and put them on his payroll, paying them with their own money, minus his cut.

Asha wasn't done with her first count when Boom got all the way on the bed and settled in behind her. He propped her hips up and pulled her panties the rest of the way down her legs. He tossed them on the floor and began to fondle her ass again. Her box instantly gushed when she looked back and saw that in addition to his shoes, he'd removed his jeans and boxers. He pulled his tee shirt off as she watched.

"What makes you happier," he asked, his voice low and carnal. "This dick or that money?"

He rubbed the fat head against her opening. She was more than ready.

"*Ooh*," she purred. "Can I have both? I never did that before."

"Did what?" he asked as he slowly penetrated her.

She inhaled sharply and couldn't immediately respond. Her eyes slipped closed as she savored every sensual sensation. "Get some dick and some money at the same time," she told him. "I never did that."

"Alright..." He began to pump his hips rhythmically, digging deep, but not too forceful, not yet. "You still counting?"

Asha's heart shuddered. She opened her eyes and couldn't remember what number she was on. Her voice was breathy when she said, "*I gotta, I gotta start over.*"

"Count out loud," he instructed her.

"*One... two... three... four... Ooh, yeah, baby...*"

Boom began to time his strokes with her count. "Four what?" he said. "It's some ones in there?"

"*Uhn, no, hundred. Five... Six... Seven... Eight... Nine... A thousand...*"

"Why you so wet?"

"*Uhn, I don't know. How wet am I?*"

"You creaming. I ain't gon' last till you get through that first stack." He kept plowing, faster now.

"This pussy making you cum?"

"You ain't right."

Asha knew he couldn't take her dirty talk. She could make him blow his load in less than five minutes if she said the right things.

"You wanna cum in my mouth, Enzo?"

"You... Ooh, fuck..."

There were people in Boom's past who knew his government name, but in their current world, Asha was the only one.

"Let me see it." She pulled away from him and turned on the mattress, still on all fours, until his dick was in her face. She saw that he wasn't lying about how wet she was. His dick was slick with her essence. The way it was bouncing, she knew he was on the verge.

She still had money gripped in both hands, so she didn't use either when she took him into her mouth. She loved the way she tasted on his dick. Boom's eyes lowered and he placed both hands on her head. He allowed her to suck him at her pace rather than fuck her face, but the result was the same. He exploded in her mouth in less than two minutes. Asha continued to feast on him until she swallowed every drop.

When he was spent, he sat back on the bed, watching her with pure satisfaction in his dark eyes. Asha crawled towards him and pushed him to his back. The look in her eyes was primal. His dick was still rock hard. She placed her hands on his chest, dropping ten thousand in the process. Boom was covered with money when she eased down onto him. He didn't complain about the dirty money as she rode him until fireworks exploded in her mind and between her legs.

"*The dick*," she said when the trembling of her legs and chest finally subsided.

Boom looked up at her with a confused expression.

"*You, uhn...*" She struggled to catch her breath. "You asked which one makes me happier, the dick or the money."

A smile spread across his face.

"We could live in a shack," Asha breathed. "Long as I got you, I don't need nothing else."

CHAPTER 8

THE COUPLE SHOWERED together and dressed. Forty minutes later, they were ready to leave to separate destinations. Boom had to go see Tomas and take care of a few other things. Asha planned to pick up a new ride – courtesy of her man – and visit a couple of people.

"You still plan on getting that bike?" Boom asked. He sat on the ottoman, putting his sneakers back on.

"Yeah." Asha pulled up the new Fireblade SP on her phone and handed it to him. The sport bike she wanted was candy apple red with blue and gray trim.

Boom frowned as he looked at the picture. "A Honda? This a bad motherfucker. You know how to ride this thing?"

"I used to have a bike before I got locked up."

"That was damn near ten years ago," Boom said as he returned her phone. "They ain't the same as they used to be. That thang you looking at can get up to 150 miles per hour."

"One eight-six," Asha corrected him.

Boom continued to frown. "I don't know how I feel about my woman on something like that. You gon' fuck around and break yo neck."

"Don't wish that bad luck on me." She sat next to him and put her shoes on.

"I never should've hooked up with a construction worker," Boom said, rising to his feet. "Yo ass got too much tomboy in you."

"I won't get it, if you don't want me to," she said seriously.

"Naw, I ain't gon' do you like that. You work hard and you deserve to get what you want. Just be careful, that's all I'm saying."

Boom didn't often show his caring nature. Each time he did, it made her heart flutter.

"I'll be careful," she promised. When she got her shoes on, she asked him, "So I just go to the dealership and they'll give me what I want?"

"Yeah," Boom said. "When you get there, ask for Mitch. I already set everything up. You gotta sign all the papers, but you ain't gotta give him nothing. You'll get the title in about a month."

Asha shook her head in wonderment. Never in her wildest dreams did she think she'd one day be able to walk out of a dealership with a brand-new vehicle without a down payment or monthly payments.

"You got some money?"

She frowned.

"Not for the bike," Boom said, "just to have in yo pocket."

"Oh. I got a few hundred."

He opened a dresser drawer and came out with a stack, about half the size of the one she was counting earlier. He placed it on the bed. "Take this. You should always have some money in your pocket."

Asha thought a few hundred *was* money, but she didn't object to having more.

"Why you treat me so good?" she asked with a smile.

"You know I care about you. Plus you earned this. Ain't like I do what I do by myself. Everything I have is yours."

Her smile deepened, but the look on Boom's face gave her pause. He approached her and took a seat on the bed. "I gotta talk to you about something."

Her expression matched his seriousness. "What's wrong?"

"It's yo cousin," Boom said. "What's his name, Tristan?"

Asha's blood ran cold. Tristan and Boom had absolutely no dealings with each other. If her cousin was on his mind, it couldn't be good news.

"Yeah, what about him?"

"He be hustling?" Boom asked.

"A little," she confirmed. "Nothing big, though. He did something wrong?"

Boom nodded. "He fucked around and got a front from one of Mr. Brown's dealers. I don't know if he fucked off the dope, or he just being an asshole, but he owe that man five thousand, and he been ducking him. They put a hit out on him. They only offering five G's, so it ain't nothing a *real* hitter would be interested in. But I'm sure somebody gon' jump on it – especially since it got something to do with Mr.

Brown. Somebody gon' wipe that boy's nose, just to get in good with him."

Asha's eyes were wide and frozen in place. "Wha, who's Mr. Brown?"

"Prolly the biggest boss in the city," Boom informed her. "He got hundreds of niggas working under him. He into everything from gun running to prostitutes and dope. If it was anybody else, I would step in and try to cool this shit down. But Mr. Brown is on a whole 'nother level. That nigga like John Gotti. Don't nobody fuck with that man. Yo cousin stupid for getting involved with anybody that got something to do with him."

Asha's mouth went dry. Next to her sister, Tristan was her closest relative.

"Wha—" She cleared her throat. "What can we do about it?"

"Tell him to pay what he owe," Boom advised her. "That's it." His eyes were stern when he said, "Don't get involved with this shit, Asha. Don't get nowhere near it. I know since you been down with this murder game, you think a bullet can solve any problem. But Mr. Brown ain't the one to fuck with. He got too many killers on his payroll. He the most dangerous man I know."

Asha was really spooked now. She thought Boom was the most dangerous man in the world. To hear him speak of another man with that level of reverence spoke volumes.

"Okay," she said. "I won't get involved. I'll talk to my cousin, tell him to pay what he owe."

"If you gotta give him that money," he said, referring to the five thousand he just gave her, "do it. It's better to pay his debt than go to his funeral."

Asha nodded. Her heart was racing. "Okay, Boom. Thanks for letting me know."

He gave her another hard look before pushing off the bed. He hefted the duffle bag and headed for the door. "A'ight. I'm out. I'll holler at you later."

CHAPTER 9

AT THE HONDA dealership, Asha hooked up with Mitch, and less than an hour later, she rolled out with the new ride she wanted. The salesman even tossed in a helmet that matched the bike's fiery red.

Before she took off, he asked her, "Do you have a leather jacket?"

Asha was all smiles as she straddled the mean machine, but you could barely make out her features behind the helmet's visor and sleek design. She shook her head.

"No, I don't have one."

"You might want to invest in one," Mitch told her. "They help protect you from flying debris, and they'll save you some skin, if you fall off your bike."

"Thanks," Asha told him. "I'll get me one."

It was mid-June, so she doubted the practicality of wearing leather in the intense Texas heat. But she'd seen a few bad road rashes and wanted no parts of that.

She made it out of the parking lot okay but nearly got tossed from her bike when she gunned it on the service road next to the dealership. Boom was right about motorcycles being a lot more powerful than the ones she rode ten years ago. It took a minute to learn that the front wheel would lift off the ground if she took off too fast. After that, the rest of the ride to her sister's house was exactly what she expected – a fun-filled adrenaline rush!

She felt like she owned the road as she zigzagged through the freeway traffic. No one could keep up with her. Her laughter was maniacal as she zoomed past the other motorists. Her bike provided enough sound effects, but she couldn't help but add her own.

"Vroom, bitches! Vroom, vroom! Get the fuck out the way!!"

CHAPTER
10

GLORIA WAS ALERTED to her sister's arrival when Asha pulled up to her house. Asha saw that her sister had also been to a dealership recently. A new Jeep Cherokee was sitting pretty in the driveway. It was black on black with a maroon interior. Asha dismounted her bike and took off her helmet. She was admiring her sister's new truck when Gloria stepped out onto the front porch.

"*Damn, sis!*" Asha said. "Look at you! This a nice ride!"

"I see you got you a new toy too," Gloria said, as she met her in the driveway. "You trying to go back to being a biker chick?"

"I was never a biker chick." Asha hugged her sister warmly when she drew near.

"Yeah, you were," Gloria said when they separated. "You used to have a few of those ugly bikes, riding around the neighborhood with your hair all wild. At least you got a helmet this time. But this bike..." She rounded the Honda, taking in the majesty of the Fireblade. "This is nothing like the ones you used to have. This is *beautiful*, Asha! It must have cost a fortune."

The bike retailed for thirty thousand, but considering Asha didn't have to save up or adjust her budget to pay for it, she felt she was being honest when she told her, "It wasn't that much." She shifted the attention to Gloria's Jeep. "What about this bad boy? I know you having fun in this thing!"

Gloria's smile was wistful. "It's a nice, smooth ride. I paid cash for it. Never did that before."

"You finally got the money from that settlement?"

Asha instantly regretted bringing up the lawsuit against the pastor who had murdered her nephew, but based on the flow of the conversation, it was probably inevitable. It had been nearly a year since Lil' Richey was abducted and brutally murdered. Pastor Butler's conviction led the way for a civil suit against him. Gloria sued for ten million, but the pastor only had a hundred thousand in assets. Last Asha had heard, Gloria's lawyer was sure they could get all of that.

Her sister nodded. Asha was glad Gloria could think about her youngest child without breaking down in tears. But the underlying despair felt like something that would never go away. Gloria's eyes remained dry, but the agony in her features was palpable and gut wrenching.

She told Asha, "We liquidated his assets. After the lawyer's cut, I got eighty thousand. I bought this Jeep and paid off me and Richard's student loans. We still got money left from Richey's life insurance."

Asha nodded solemnly. "I still think you should go after the church. I read about that pastor having a pattern of behavior. They didn't do nothing about it. You could get millions, if you sue them."

"My lawyer thinks so too. I haven't decided yet. I might let her draft a letter, see if they wanna settle out of court. If they do, I'll probably take whatever they give me. I don't wanna fight no more. That civil trial was worse than the criminal one. I can't keep going through this, just to get more money."

Asha understood that. She stepped to her sister and hugged her again. "I love you. It'll get better."

"I know it will," Gloria said and returned the affection. When she backed away, she said, "Asha, it's something I been wanting to talk to you about. Can you be honest with me?"

"Yeah, sis. What's up?"

Gloria's expression shifted from forlorn to accusatory. "I want you to tell me what's going on with you. I know you said you were taking some time off after Richey died, but Mr. Luck says you quit your job a long time ago. You don't come around as much as you used to. You moved in with some man, but you don't never bring him around. And now you pull up in this bike... What have you gotten yourself into? You got a new job you haven't told me about?"

Asha's face burned. She couldn't believe her sister called her old boss. Gloria and Boom were two people she always found it hard to lie to. "I'm working," she offered.

"What kind of work? You still doing construction?"

Asha shook her head. "No. It's... It's different."

Gloria pursed her lips and nodded. "It's something illegal, ain't it?"

"Why it gotta be that?"

"If you can't be honest with me, then just tell me to mind my business," she snapped, growing frustrated. "But I care about you, and I'm worried. I don't want you to end up back in prison."

Asha sighed. "Okay, sis. It's uh, I mean, it ain't on the up and up, but it's not that bad."

Gloria sighed heavily. Thinking about Richey didn't bring her to tears, but her sister's troubles did.

"Asha, why would you do that – after all you been through? I was up at that prison once a week when you got locked up. We cried together. You promised you would never do anything that would get you sent back to that place."

"I'm not going back," Asha said. "I'm telling you, it's not that bad."

"Is it drugs?"

"No," Asha said forcefully. "You know I ain't never been down with that."

"Then you're stealing from people..."

Asha shook her head. "No. It ain't that either."

Gloria brought a hand to her face and rubbed her temple. "You not gon' tell me, are you?"

Asha continued to shake her head. "I'm sorry, sis. I can't. But I ain't gon' be doing it for that long. It's just a little thing I got going on for now."

"It's got something to do with that man you with?"

Asha shook her head again, but her eyes betrayed her. The tears began to roll down Gloria's cheeks.

She told her, "It hurts me to say this, Asha, but you know I love you. If Mama was still here, she'd give you the same tough love. When you got locked up, I stood by you, because it wasn't your fault. That man tried to rape you, and you defended yourself.

"But what you're doing now is not the same. You're making a choice to do something illegal. I think you got yourself caught up with a criminal, and you done fell right in line with him. If you need to come stay with us to get away from him and get your life back together, you know you're welcome.

"But if you continue on this path and get locked up again, don't bother calling me. I'm not driving three hours to and three more hours from that prison every Saturday for another ten or however many years they give you this time. Right now, you got a chance to make the right decision. If you choose not to, you *deserve* to get locked up again." Her eyes were cold when she added, "That's probably the best thing for you. Lord knows I don't want you to end up dead."

She turned and headed for the house without another word. When she disappeared inside, Asha struggled to keep her own emotions under control as she put her helmet on and mounted her bike.

The Fireblade was a lot less fun when she got back on the road, heading south.

CHAPTER
11

SHE ARRIVED AT Tristan's apartment fifteen minutes later. He answered the door wearing only his boxers.

He wiped the sleep from his eyes and offered a groggy, "What's up?"

Asha reached for the doorknob and yanked it closed. "Nigga, put some motherfucking clothes on!" she shouted through the door.

She heard him laughing on the other side. "A'ight, Asha."

She frowned as she waited on the breezeway. Two minutes later, Tristan emerged again, this time wearing jeans and a tee shirt.

He told his baby-mama, "I'll be right back."

"You leaving?" Courtney asked.

"Naw. I ain't got no shoes on. I'ma step outside for a minute and talk to my cousin."

He closed the door and grinned at Asha. Tristan was caramel colored. He'd always been a pretty boy, but he thugged up his appearance when he got older with long hair and a collection of tats on his arms and chest.

He noticed the helmet Asha toted and asked, "You back to riding bikes?"

"Yeah," she replied. "I picked one up today."

"It's down there?" he asked, looking towards the parking lot. "I wanna check it out."

"In a minute," Asha said. "I wanna ask you about something first."

He leaned against the railing, facing her. "What's up?"

She cut straight to the chase. "Word on the streets is you owe a man five stacks, and you ain't paying. Now he offering that same amount to take you out."

Tristan frowned. He waited a few beats before asking, "Where you hear that from?"

She regarded him coldly. "It don't matter where I heard it from. Is it true?" Before he could answer, she said, "You know what, I ain't finna give you a chance to lie about it. I just wanna know why you did that dumb-ass shit."

Tristan smacked his lips. "That nigga ain't finna do shit. I told him I was gon' pay him."

"That nigga ain't finna do shit? You know he work for Mr. Brown, right?"

Asha had just learned of the crime boss, but she tossed his name around like she had all the intel. Tristan's eyes narrowed.

"Yeah, but he ain't a higher up. He just some hood nigga. This ain't got nothing to do with Mr. Brown."

Asha stepped to him. "Listen, I'ma need you to stop trying to act like you hard and then turn around talking like you as green as AstroTurf. If a nigga work for Mr. Brown, and you fuck over that nigga, then you fucking over Mr. Brown. I know you know that ain't something you wanna do."

Tristan grimaced. "How you even know about this shit?"

"Don't worry about it."

He sighed. "Asha, I'm telling you it ain't like you thinking."

"And I'm telling you they done greenlighted yo ass. You got that man's money or not?"

"Yeah." He looked away. "Some of it."

"How much more you need?" Asha asked, reaching inside her purse.

Tristan's eyes grew large when he saw the stack she produced. "You serious, huh?"

She looked up at him. "I'm serious about trying to save your life. How much do you need, Tristan."

He shrugged. He was sheepish when he said, "I owe him five racks."

Asha couldn't hide her annoyance. "You telling me you ain't got none of it?"

He shook his head.

"I ought'a kick yo ass," she said as she shoved the money in his chest. "Talking about you gon' pay that man, and you ain't got a dime of it. *Here*."

Tristan was uneasy, but he took the money. "Where you get this from?"

"Don't worry about it." She turned and headed for the stairs.

"Wait."

She didn't stop for him. He caught up with her when she got on her bike. His eyes bugged as he admired the ride.

"*Goddamn, cuz.* You rolling like this?"

"Gone, Tristan. You done pissed me off."

"I'm sorry, Asha. I appreciate you helping me. For real. I didn't know what I was gon' do."

She continued to fume, but her features softened. "It's okay. Just pay that man and don't fuck with him no mo'."

"Alright," he said, then, "Hey, it's something I wanted to ask you about."

"What?"

He stepped closer. In a conspiratorial tone, he asked, "You still fucking with Boom?"

She frowned. "Why you ask me that?"

"I heard he was running with a new girl. They been *real* busy. She go by Brionna. *Brionna Boom.* She light skinned..."

Asha's heart froze. "Somebody think it's me?"

"Naw. I was just wondering because the way they describe her made me think of you."

Her frown returned. "You told somebody that?"

"Hell naw. I'm just saying, you got this money, and you rolling around on this new bike..."

"Tristan, you know I don't fuck with Boom after that shit that went down with Lil' Richey. What I look like hooking up with that nigga?"

He nodded. "That's what I figured, but I thought I might as well ask."

"Whatever," she said and put her helmet on.

Through the visor, she could tell her cousin wasn't fully convinced. She started her bike and peeled off, hoping that was the last she'd hear of his debt and his accusation.

CHAPTER
12

LATER THAT NIGHT, Asha met one of her old coworkers at a bar on the west side of town. She wasn't a fan of honkytonks or biker bars, but she had a new bike, and Murray was a frequent patron of the Red Rooster. He met her outside of the establishment, thinking she might feel more comfortable there if she was greeted by a familiar face. But Asha wasn't fearful of the rednecks on that side of town. They may have been on edge because their Confederate monuments were coming down, but they'd be in for a rude awakening if they stepped to Boom's girl the wrong way.

When Murray saw her Honda, his jaw dropped. His eyes grew by the same degrees.

"*Holy fuck!*" he exclaimed when Asha parked and removed her helmet.

Murray was ten years older and as country as a bowl of grits. He wore jeans and boots that had seen better days. Asha still had on the jeans, tee shirt and sneakers she put on earlier that day. Judging by the looks of the bar, she didn't think she was under dressed.

"Damn, girl. I missed you!" Murray gave her a big hug. She'd worked with him for two years at Victory Awnings. In all that time, he'd never greeted her like that.

"I missed you too," she told him.

Despite his rough appearance, Murray was fresh smelling. Asha detected Old Spice cologne. His attention returned to her bike.

"This brand new?" he asked, circling it.

"Yeah," she said, beaming. "Just got it today."

He whistled, shaking his head. "I bet this sumbitch can go!"

"Fastest thing I ever been on," Asha confirmed. "Wanna take it for a ride?"

"Hell yeah! You don't mind?"

"No, but be careful with the take off. I damn near got tossed the first time I got on it."

"I will," he said, taking the keys from her. He gingerly got on the bike and looked around for the ignition. "How the hell I turn this thing on?"

Asha showed him and then backed away when he got it started.

He waited for her to hop on behind him and then asked, "You ain't coming?"

"Naw, go ahead. You gonna wear your helmet?"

"Hell no! I want people to see me on this thang!"

Murray couldn't stop grinning as he backed out of the parking spot and took off down the street. Asha waited nearly ten minutes for him to return. His smile was as big as ever. He parked the bike and hopped off.

"I love my old Harley," he said as he returned the keys, "but I wouldn't mind getting something like that one day. I know it set you back a pretty penny."

"They don't come cheap," Asha agreed.

They entered the Red Rooster and headed straight for the bar. Asha wasn't bothered about being the only black person in the building. She collected a few curious stares, but there's some truth to the adage that Texas is one of the friendliest states. A few cowboys tipped their hats to her, which was something she didn't think she'd ever experienced.

Midway through their first round, Murray asked her, "So how's things going in your world? Do you miss the old crew at work?"

"Yeah," Asha said reflectively. "I really do. You and Mr. Luck for sure."

"Everybody's wondering what you been up to since you left. You looking good," he said, looking her up and down. "I always thought you were too pretty to be in construction, but you got a new glow to you. Don't look like you been spending too much time in this goddamn heat."

Murray had been happily married for almost two decades, so Asha knew he wasn't flirting.

"You're right; I don't do construction no more," she told him. "Got me an office job. My sister hooked me up."

One of his eyebrows raised. "No shit?"

"Yup. I'm sitting on my ass most of the day in a cubicle. Under the air conditioner... I even got a little fan next to my monitor."

Murray rolled his eyes. "Oh yeah, go ahead and rub in it!"

Asha laughed. "I'm just kidding. But it is better than being outside, up on them ladders all day. Can you believe I haven't had a cut or scrape on my hands since I quit?"

"Hell yeah, I can believe it." He showed her his hands. They were big and rough with a fresh Band-Aid on his index finger. "Just got this new war wound today. Went all the way down to the white meat."

"*Ooh*. I'm sorry."

"It's nothing. All in a day's work."

They shot the shit for a while longer before Asha got a call on her cellphone. She frowned when she saw her cousin's name on the Caller ID. "What's up?" she answered.

"*Asha!*" Tristan's voice was high and panicked. He sounded like he was on the road.

Asha's eyes narrowed as she turned away from her friend. "What's up?" she said again. "What's wrong with you?"

"*Somebody following me*," Tristan reported. "*I think these niggas trying to kill me*! They been on my ass for five minutes. Everywhere I turn, they turn. They waiting for me to stop somewhere, so they can get me. I know it! These niggas trying to snatch me!"

"Wait, slow down," Asha said. "I'll be right back," she told Murray before slipping off her stool. She couldn't find a quiet spot in the bar, so she stepped outside.

"Where you at?" she asked Tristan. "Who following you?"

He told her, "I think it's them niggas we was talking about. The one I owe is named Mook. I can't tell if it's him in the car behind me, but I know it got something to do with him. Cuz, I'm scared as hell. I ain't got no strap on me or nothing. I don't know what the fuck to do."

Asha's eyebrows were knitted together. "But you paid him, right?"

"No, not yet. I was going to but–"

"Tristan, I swear to God I'ma kick yo ass if you fucked off that money I gave you. Why you ain't pay that man, like I told you?"

"I'm telling you, I was gonna pay him. I just had to take care of a few things first. I texted him and told him I'd give it to him tomorrow."

"*Tomorrow*? *I told you they greenlighted yo ass, and you still fucking around*? I see why they coming for yo dumb ass!"

She was about to ask what he expected her to do about this when he told her, "*Cuz, I'm scared to death.*" He sounded like he was near tears, or already crying. "I know you said you ain't Brionna, but if you is, or if it's *anythang* you can do to help me, *please Asha*. I need you bad. These niggas gon' kill me!"

Asha was furious. Every word that came out of her cousin's mouth made her more upset. She should probably leave him to his own devices, but as dumb and wrong as he was, he was still family. She knew Boom wouldn't support her decision to intervene, but that was because he became a loner once he got into their current lifestyle. Maybe he had forgotten what it was like to have blood relatives who depended on you.

"Where you at?" Asha growled.

"I'm on the south. I keep driving, but sooner or later they gon' realize I'm going in circles."

"Keep driving," Asha told him. "I'm headed that way. I'll call you back in a minute."

"*Dammit!*" she said when she disconnected. Her adrenaline rush was laced with dread. If Tristan didn't have two small children at home, she might have taken her ass back to the bar and wished him luck. Or maybe not. After what happened with Gloria earlier that day, Asha had a fresh understanding of the importance of family.

She returned to the bar long enough to apologize to Murray for having to cut their time together short, and then she rushed back to her bike. Thankfully, the Red Rooster was right off the interstate. Two minutes later, Asha was flying down the freeway, trying to see how fast her Fireblade could really go.

CHAPTER 13

ASHA'S BLOOD WAS flowing hot and hard by the time she made it to the south side. She didn't try to use her cellphone while she was on the freeway, but she called her cousin back as soon as she took the East Berry exit and had to stop at a light. She took the call on a Bluetooth earpiece under her helmet.

"*Cuz!*" Tristan answered. "*Damn, Asha, I thought you wasn't gon' call back*! I was finna drive to the police station to get these niggas off me!"

Asha was a hundred percent against snitching, especially self-snitching, but if it saved her cousin's life and kept her out of it, maybe that wasn't a bad idea.

"Why you ain't do it?" she asked him.

"'Cause I got some warrants," Tristan told her. "And I'm riding dirty. I got some dope in the trunk. I'ma get locked up, if they search my car."

Asha knew that not only would he be in jail, but the other inmates would soon learn he was a rat. He was as good as dead on the streets and behind bars.

"*Please tell me you close,*" Tristan cried.

"I'm close," Asha said. "I'm turning on Berry now."

"I can't hardly hear you!" Tristan shouted.

Asha couldn't do anything about her bike's powerful and noisy engine, so she had to raise her voice. "*I'm on Berry! Where you at, Tristan?*"

"*I'm over here on Bideker!*"

That was only a few minutes away. Asha started to book it in that direction, but she thought it would be better if he came to her, rather than try to keep up with every turn he was making. She pulled into the parking lot of a convenience store on Riverside Drive and left the engine running.

"Come towards Riverside and Berry," she instructed. "I'll–"

BAM!

The collision on the other end of the line was so loud, Asha felt like a wreck had occurred right behind her.

"Tristan, what–"

"*They hit me!*" her cousin squealed. "*They ran into the back of me! It's Mook in the car! They trying to run me off the road! Damn, cousin, they finna kill me!*"

Asha's heart was going a mile a minute, but she implored him to, "Calm down! Is your car alright? Can you keep driving?"

"*Yeah, but they... Oh, my God! What the fuck, man? What the fuck?!*"

"*Tristan, keep driving!*" she barked. "Can you make it to Riverside and Berry?"

"*Yeah, I'm almost there!*"

Asha heard tires squealing.

"What's gon' happen?" Tristan wanted to know. "What you gon' do?"

Asha hadn't decided yet, but the next sound she heard made up her mind.

POP!POP! POP! POP!

"*They shooting!*" Tristan screamed.

Asha's body went numb. Not only did she hear the gunshots through her Bluetooth, but she heard them down the street. She looked in that direction and saw her cousin's late model Buick speeding in her direction. Another car, a much newer and faster one, was right on his tail.

"*They shooting!*"

"Keep coming," Asha said, her voice calm now. "I see you..."

Her heart didn't beat at all as she pulled a black Sig Sauer from beneath her shirt. She cocked it but left the safety on before returning it to the holster.

"*Cuz, where are you?*" Tristan cried.

He sped through the intersection, running a red light. The car pursuing him did the same. As they passed, Asha saw that he was being chased by a faster Toyota Supra. Tristan had no chance of outrunning them. She was surprised the goons were willing to wreck their sleek ride during the pursuit.

"*I'm right behind you!*" Asha told her cousin as she sped out of the parking lot.

She doubted if Tristan could hear her over the squeal of her tires, but it didn't matter at that point. She quickly weaved through the traffic and caught up with the Toyota, just as the passenger leaned out of the window and let off more shots.

POP!POP!POP!

Asha saw the back window on her cousin's Buick crack into a thousand tiny pieces, but it held its shape and didn't fall from the frame. Tristan's car swerved violently to the left, into oncoming traffic. Asha's eyes widened. She thought he'd taken a headshot, but he righted his car before colliding into the curb or any of the cars heading in the opposite direction.

"**ASHA**!" he screamed into her earpiece.

"**Are you hit**?"

She couldn't make out his response. She kicked her bike into another gear and easily pulled alongside the Supra. The driver looked over at her. His eyes registered confusion. Rather than assume the worst and run her off the road, like Boom would've done, the man focused on his driving. His eyes returned to Tristan's Buick. Before he had a chance to look her way again, Asha skillfully drew her weapon, maintaining control of the bike with one hand. She aimed, flipped off the safety and fired into the car with one fluid motion.

BLAT!BLAT! BLAT!BLAT!BLAT!

Her nostrils flared as she watched the carnage up close. The driver's face and chest exploded in a cloud of blood. She was sure she hit the passenger too, but his demise was not confirmed. Rather than veer in either direction, the Supra simply slowed in the middle of the street.

Asha and Tristan continued south. She was right behind him now. She returned her pistol to the holster and did everything Boom would've wanted her to; she checked to see how the witnesses were responding and mapped out the quickest route to the freeway. They were deeper in the neighborhood now. If she stopped at every light, which was the safest option, it would take her five minutes to get back to the interstate.

"*Asha*!"

"Calm down," she told her cousin. "I'm right behind you. You safe, for now."

"That was you?" he asked. "You shot 'em?"

Asha wouldn't dare confirm something like that over the phone, but she knew Tristan wasn't very street smart.

"You got somewhere safe to go?" she asked him.

"Yeah, I uh, I think I can find somewhere."

"You need to lay low till you hear from me again," she told him.

"Okay. It's um…" He struggled to catch his breath. "It's, it's you, ain't it? You her? You Brionna…"

This nigga dumb as a box of rocks.

"Tristan, don't ask me no more motherfucking questions! Just go somewhere safe, and don't tell nobody where you at except Courtney!"

She was glad they were nearing a light. She dug her phone from her pocket and hung up on him. Tristan made a right turn at the intersection, but Asha had to wait for the light to change before she turned left. Before she put her phone away, it vibrated in her hand. She cringed when she saw that it was Boom.

Fuck.

She sighed as she took the call.

"Hey, baby."

"Hey," he said. "Where you be?"

"I'm, uh, I'm on the south." The light changed, and she got moving.

"You on yo bike? I can't hardly hear you."

"Yeah. I'm on the road."

"What's wrong?"

She bit the bullet and told him, "I had to intervene in my cousin's lil' issue. I left a couple of dollars on the table." That was their code for dead bodies.

She hoped Boom wasn't able to hear her well, but he was immediately furious.

"*Goddammit, girl, I told you to leave that shit alone*! That nigga damn sure gon' get got now. You ain't did nothing but prolong the inevitable – and put yourself in danger! You need to bring yo ass home – now!"

Disappointing her man was the worst feeling in the world. Asha dreaded going home to him, but she knew he would forgive her and figure out a way to make things right.

The sound of tires squealing snapped her out of her self-pity and made the hairs stand on her arms. She looked back and saw a car racing towards her.

"*Aww, shit*," she told Boom. "It's somebody behind me."

"It's the laws?"

"Naw, it's... *Aww fuck*!"

She had to gun her bike to avoid getting rear-ended. Her bike was fast, but the roaring engine behind her was just as speedy.

"***Asha***!"

She could barely hear her man over the high-pitched sound of burning rubber – her tires and the car behind her.

"***Where are you***?!" Boom screamed.

She shouted the location, but she couldn't even hear her own voice. There was no way Boom would understand what she was saying.

PART TWO
DOLLARS ON THE TABLE

CHAPTER 14

ASHA DIDN'T THINK it was a witness or even a vigilante on her tail. Whoever it was was too invested in the outcome. They didn't simply want to obtain her license plate number, so they could contact the authorities. They wanted to apprehend her – or worse. She couldn't rule out an off-duty police officer.

Whatever the case, she wasn't confident about her chances of outrunning them. She risked a look back while cutting a corner so hard she nearly drifted into the curb. She saw that the car chasing her was a Porsche 911. As speedy as her Fireblade was, she knew the Porsche was faster. Her advantage was maneuverability.

"*Asha*!"

Boom continued to scream into her earpiece. She did her best to respond to him, but her revving engine and screeching tires kicked up so much racket, she couldn't make out what he was saying. She prayed he could hear some of what she was trying to tell him.

Her blood raced through her veins as she yelled, "*I'm on the south side! I'm trying to get to the freeway, but this nigga on my ass!*"

"*Where you at?!*" Boom bellowed. "*I'ma come to you! Can you make it to the freeway? Try to get on the freeway and outrun 'em!*"

Asha didn't hear any of that. Her goal was to lose the tail before she got to the interstate, but the Porsche's driver seemed to be an expert wheelman, and this was her first day on a bike in ten years. The dark south side streets ranged from sparsely to moderately populated. Asha bent another corner and found herself on a street with a multitude of cars parked on both sides. She skated between them with no problem. She hoped the Porsche would have to slow down, at least a little.

"*I'm on Hattie!*" she yelled, "*about to turn on Illinois!* **Oh shit**!"

She overestimated her bike's braking power when she cut the next corner. The Fireblade began to slide treacherously towards the curb. She was leaning so hard, her knee nearly scraped the street.

SCUUUUUURRRRR!!

"*Asha!*"

She righted herself at the last possible second, but had almost come to a complete stop. Behind her, she saw that the Porsche hadn't lost any ground at all. In fact, it was starting to gain on her.

She gunned it again, leaning forward to help keep the front wheel from lifting from the pavement. Her bike howled like a banshee.

VREEEEEEEEEN!

"Get on the freeway!" Boom yelled. *"I'm in the car, fifteen minutes away!"*

Asha heard none of that. She told him, *"I can't lose 'em! They still on my ass!"*

She hit another corner, a little slower this time, and managed to maintain most of her speed. The Porsche came flying around the same intersection. It drifted perfectly, and then the driver slammed his foot on the gas. The mean machine bucked like a bronco and began to eat up the distance between them.

"Motherfucker!" Asha growled.

She raced another few blocks before bending another corner. She used her momentary advantage to take a stand. She stopped in the middle of the new street and drew her weapon. The moment the Porsche rounded the corner, she let him have it.

BLAT!BLAT!BLAT!BLAT!BLAT!

"Asha!"

"That was me!" she told her man.

Her clip empty, she quickly returned the piece to the holster. She saw that at least of couple of her shots rang true. The Porsche's front windshield had taken damage. Her eyes widened when she saw that the motherfucker was still coming!

"Goddammit!"

She punched it again, but her attempt to gain the upper hand turned out to be her downfall. She couldn't accelerate quickly enough to best the Porsche, which was in full stride. Two blocks down the road, she tried to hit another corner, and her luck ran out. Through her sideview mirrors, she saw the Porsche's headlights closing in on her.

The roar of the sport car's engine was so loud, she felt it rumbling in her chest.

BAM!

The car impacted her bike with enough force to send her flying towards the lawn of Mt. Carmel Baptist Church. Asha didn't have time to scream or reflect on the fact that a leather jacket may not have been so impractical after all in the short time she was airborne. She impacted the hard earth with enough force to knock the senses and consciousness from her, despite her helmet.

As jarring as the collision was, she felt no pain as all understanding of space and time was suddenly snatched from her.

CHAPTER
15

BOOM WAS ALREADY on the freeway when he heard the gunshots and the crash. His eyes were frantic. He gripped the steering wheel so hard, his fingertips were cold. He hadn't been able to hear much of what Asha was saying during her harrowing ride, but after the collision, things became deathly quiet. He tried again.

"Asha! You alright?"

No response.

"Them motherfuckers..."

Boom's nostrils flared as he gritted his teeth. Everything in his field of vision was tinted with murderous, bloody red. He doubted if he would be able to find his woman with the vague descriptions she'd given him, but the south side wasn't very expansive, and it was his only lead.

As he drove, he realized the Bluetooth Asha was wearing had not been disabled during the impact. The speakers in his SUV picked up the sound of a motor running and voices in the distance. Gradually the voices became more decipherable, as the assailants moved closer to his woman.

"... but that bitch can move. Thought you was gonna lose her."

"Fuck naw."

"Thought you was done for when she turned around and started busting."

"Shit, me too. You think Fizz gon' make it?"

"I don't know. Nigga bleeding like a motherfucker. We prolly gon' have to let him bleed out, dump him somewhere. I'ma tell 'em I'm taking him to the hospital though, give him some hope."

"You a cold motherfucker."

Boom's eyes narrowed as he mentally recorded every word of their conversation. He heard rustling on Asha's end of the line, and then one of them said, "You think she dead?"

"I don't know," his cohort responded. A few moments later, "Naw, she still breathing. Get her helmet off. Let's see if it's her."

"Nigga, you know it's her. You seen the way she..."

Their voices were lost again when the rustling on their end of the line became even louder, presumably as they took Asha's helmet off.

Things became quiet again, and then one of them said, "Is that her?"

"I ain't never seen Brionna," his cohort replied. "But from what I heard, I'm pretty sure this that bitch. Grab her legs."

"Hold up... You see that?"

"What?"

"In her ear."

More rustling.

Boom hoped they'd take the Bluetooth with them, possibly in the front seat of their car, so he could continue to eavesdrop on their conversation. But the line abruptly went dead.

It didn't feel like he'd breathed the whole time the men were talking. Boom took a deep breath and tried to calm his nerves. His exhalation was hot lava. His rage had reached epic, self-destructive levels. But he knew patience and cunning was what he needed to get his woman back safely. Finding a balance between his battling demons would take every bit of his willpower.

CHAPTER 16

WHEN HE ARRIVED on the south side, Boom reached out to a trusted resource. JB picked up after a couple of rings.

"What it do?"

Boom was never one for small talk. "Need you to get on yo scanner," he told him. "Can you get on a south side frequency? Tell me what you hear."

"For sho'," his friend said. "Anythang in particular you looking for? You know the south always jumping this time of night; assaults, robberies, prostitutes…"

"I'm looking for accidents," Boom told him, "and maybe a murder."

JB did not question why he wanted the information. He told him, "Bet. Hold the line."

Boom pulled in the parking lot of a McDonald's while he waited. He didn't have time to work on a disguise before he rushed out of the house, but he always had a few things handy in whatever vehicle he was traveling in. In the center console, he found a Ziplock bag with what appeared to be a fistful of hair inside. He opened it and affixed the carefully crafted goatee to his face. Without turning on the lights to make sure it was on properly, he knew it might be a little crooked. But it was dark outside, and he didn't expect too much scrutiny.

He would've preferred some type of wig, but he had to settle for a ballcap and a pair of glasses. He checked his visor mirror and thought his disguise was passable. Some might consider it exceptional.

JB came back to the phone and said, "Nigga, the south is on fire tonight! You got a double homicide on Riverside and four accidents."

Boom did not react to his woman's handiwork. He asked him, "Any of those accidents involve a motorcycle?"

"Yeah, that's the one getting the most attention. Wasn't nobody on the scene when the laws got there, only the bike. They looking for whoever was on the bike plus whoever hit 'em."

"Gimme the address on the murders and the bike."

JB gave him the information, and Boom told him, "A'ight. 'Preciate it." He disconnected and headed for the first crime scene.

CHAPTER 17

AS EXPECTED, THE location of the double homicide drew a large crowd, both from the police and bystanders. Detectives blocked off the area in a two-block radius. Boom parked nearby and exited his vehicle. He approached the onlookers and blended in with them, getting as close as he could to the police cars that halted traffic and redirected motorists.

From his vantage point, he could see a Toyota Supra was the main focus of the investigation. The people he was mingling with didn't have much information, but a talkative crackhead sounded like he had arrived on the scene shortly after the first police car arrived.

"You seen what happened?" Boom asked him.

"Uh-uhn." The disheveled man looked Boom up and down. "Who is you?"

"I ain't nobody," Boom told him. "Just trying to drive through, and they got this fucking road shut down."

"It's some bodies in that car," the addict told him. His eyes were big, his voice spooky. "Somebody blast them niggas while they was driving."

"No shit?"

"Yeah. Prolly over some dope or something."

"Anybody know who did it?"

He shook his head. "Don't nobody know shit. I heard it was somebody in the backseat that did it; shot both of 'em and then bailed."

Boom knew that theory wouldn't hold up once the detectives traced the trajectory of the shots, but it didn't appear anyone thought a motorcycle was involved, and that was good news.

The second address JB had given him led Boom to Mt. Carmel Baptist Church. The police blocked traffic in this area too, but there were only two squad cars at this location, rather than the dozen at the double homicide. Boom was able to walk all the way to the bike's skid marks before an officer stopped him.

"Hey, you can't come over here. There was an accident."

"That's what I'm trying to find out about," Boom told him. "My homeboy took off on his bike about an hour ago. He was high than a motherfucker. Ain't nobody been able to get in touch with him. I heard a bike crashed over here, and I wanted to know if it was him."

That piqued the officer's interest. "What kind of bike does your friend drive?"

"It's a black Kawasaki."

"It ain't him," the cop said.

"How you know it ain't him?"

"Because the bike that crashed over here isn't a black Kawasaki."

"You just trying to get me to leave," Boom pressed. "Lemme see."

He played the role of an ignorant black man so successfully, the cop was more irritated than offended by the intrusion.

"I told you it ain't him." He stepped aside for a second and pointed to the motorcycle lying next to the curb. "Does that bike look black to you?"

Boom fought to hide his reaction to the sight of Asha's wrecked Honda. It was hard to believe she had just bought the bike today. He never even got the chance to see her riding it. Now the Fireblade looked inoperable. It didn't seem possible for her to survive the crash without major injuries, but the men who abducted her said she was alive and didn't mention any obvious physical trauma. He had to find solace in that.

"Naw, that ain't his bike," Boom told the cop.

"Thank you. Now if you don't mind, we're busy over here."

Boom returned to his vehicle and slowly drove away.

CHAPTER 18

HE HADN'T LEFT the south side when he received a call on a phone he hadn't used all month. He retrieved it from the glove compartment, surprised the battery hadn't gone dead. He recognized the number but had no idea why Milton was contacting him.

"What's up?" he answered.

"Hey, uh, it's somebody wanna talk to you," Milton said. "I ain't tell him nothing about you. I told him I don't know shit. But he asked if I knew how to get in contact with you, and I told him I'd try. If you don't wanna talk to him, just say the word, and I'll tell him I couldn't reach you."

Milton had every right to be fearful. Boom had been known to do bad things to associates who helped strangers get in touch with him.

"Who is it?" he asked, his voice menacing.

Milton told him, "It's Mr. Brown."

Boom's blood ran cold. He wasn't usually one to lose his cool, but he had to pull over for a moment. He considered the repercussions of taking the call. The phone

Milton had contacted him on was a throwaway, so there was no worry there. Boom could think of no danger that would come his way if he spoke to Mr. Brown, so he told him, "Go ahead. Give him this number."

He disconnected and waited two minutes before the phone rang again. While he sat there, he contemplated Asha's fate, if he didn't say the right things when the kingpin called him. He considered all of the horrible things he would do if they hurt her. He was still parked on the side of the road when he answered.

"Yeah."

"You know who this is?" the man on the other end asked. His voice was deep and gravelly, like the idling engine of an eighteen-wheeler.

"This Mr. Brown?" Boom asked. He had never spoken to the man directly. He wouldn't consider himself intimidated by the boss' reputation, but he certainly respected it.

"Yeah, this is Mr. Brown. Before you get all hotheaded, I'm sure you already know we got yo girl. Things already bad, but they can get a lot worse. Now I'ma tell you how this is gonna go down..."

CHAPTER 19

BOOM REMINDED HIMSELF that patience and cunning would be the key to this conundrum and was able to maintain his cool while speaking to the notorious Mr. Brown.

"You gonna tell me how it's gonna go?" he asked.

"Yeah, that's right, Boom."

"Alright. Go ahead."

"I'm gonna hold on to yo gal, until I settle my business with her cousin," the man said. "After that, I'm willing to give her back, but I want a mil', and I gotta teach her a lesson first."

"Teach her a lesson?"

"Yeah. Don't worry, you'll get her back in the same condition you last seen her, more or less."

More or less?

"But she won't be able to play her little sneak game no more," Mr. Brown continued. "Everyone who sees her will immediately know who she is."

Boom seethed. Mr. Brown could be referring to anything from a missing limb to a missing nose.

"That ain't gon' work," he told him. "I don't care what you do to her cousin, but you not gon' lay a hand on my girl. I understand she was out of line, but I'm not finna let another nigga discipline my woman."

After a pause, Mr. Brown said, "I understand why you feel that way. But I'm sure you understand the streets is watching. She killed two, maybe three of my people. I can't let her go with no repercussions."

"Them people you talking about ain't worth a million dollars," Boom said. "Ain't nobody on your team worth that much."

"You don't get to decide how much my people are worth. You telling me you ain't gon' pay?"

"I thought we were trying to have a real conversation. What you talking about is extortion."

The man chuckled. "Okay, tell me what you think is a better offer."

"I done already told you. You take care of your business with her cousin and let my woman go. I'll deal with her for what she did. I can take care of your men's funerals, but I ain't giving you a million dollars."

The crime lord considered that before saying, "Nah, I like my plan better. You over there talking like you got the upper hand, when you know that ain't the case. You need to think long and hard about this. I know you a solid hitter, but you only one man. I got a goddamn army. I got hundreds of hitters."

Boom was unfazed. "And I'ma bury every last one of them, if you don't release my girl tonight. When they all gone, I'ma come for you, Mr. Brown. You need to think long and hard about that."

"You have any idea who you talking to?"

"Yeah, I know exactly who you are. And I'm done talking. I better have my girl in my house tonight, or tomorrow it's gon' get *real bloody*."

He disconnected. Boom's eyes were transfixed but unfocused on the road ahead of him. All he saw was red. He wasn't sure if he'd made the right move, but he felt Mr. Brown had given him no choice. The kingpin was right about one thing: The streets were indeed watching. He couldn't allow Mr. Brown to extort him or maim Asha. He understood the decision may cost her her life, but he had a few more cards to play.

He put his truck in drive and got moving. While he drove, he called the man who initially told him about the bounty on Tristan's head. Perm sounded wary when he answered the phone.

"Hey, what's up?"

"You remember telling me about that $5,000 hit they put out on that boy who owed one of Mr. Brown's men?"

"Yeah, Tristan?"

"That's him," Boom said. "I need you to give me his address."

"That's – um... I heard it was some killings tonight on the south. That got something to do with all this?"

"Why you asking me?"

"'Cause I don't want no part of it, if that's what's going on."

"It sounds like you telling me you ain't gon' give me the address," Boom said. "Is that what you saying?"

"Naw, I ain't saying that. I don't even know where that nigga stay. I'm just saying, I don't want nothing to do with no killings."

"I'ma be straight with you, Perm. I don't believe you don't know where Tristan stay. If I gotta come over there and ask you face-to-face, you ain't gon' like it."

"What? Naw, man. *Don't come over here*! I think he stay in the Falcon Crest Apartments on Evergreen. But I don't know the apartment number."

Boom knew the area. He made a left and headed in that direction, but he told Perm, "I'm on my way to yo place. I'm ten minutes away. If you don't call me back with an apartment number before I knock on yo door, then we gon' have to have that lil' face-to-face."

"Man, why you wanna come over here? I ain't do shit to you! I don't got shit to do with this!"

"You ain't gotta be in it, if you give me that apartment number. Otherwise, I'll see you in a little bit." He disconnected.

Five minutes later, Perm called him back. "It's apartment 212. Now leave me outta this shit!"

"Watch yo mouth," Boom growled. "Act like you know who you talking to."

"I'm sorry, Boom. But I don't know why you charging me up over something I ain't got nothing to do with. This shit ain't right."

"Quit crying, nigga. I'm sorry for coming at you like that, but I ain't in a good mood right now. I appreciate yo help."

"Alright. You welcome, man."

Boom disconnected and drove the rest of the way to Falcon Crest in silence. His mind was going a mile a minute. He was close to putting a few of the pieces together, but he was a long way from a final solution.

CHAPTER 20

NO ONE ANSWERED the door of apartment 212, but before he knocked, Boom heard children's voices inside. He thought he heard a female trying to quiet them. He hated to go hard on people Asha cared about, but time was of the essence.

He checked his surroundings before drawing his pistol. There was no one on the breezeway, but there were lights on in the neighbor's apartments. If he didn't play his cards right, the police would be on the scene within a few minutes. He weighed his options and decided he had no other choice.

He easily breached the entrance with a hard kick next to the doorknob.

BOOMP!

He immediately heard screaming inside. He entered the apartment and followed the voices to one of the bedrooms. He appeared in the doorway with his pistol drawn. Thankfully the young woman huddled in a corner gripped an infant and a toddler, rather than a weapon of her own. Boom surveyed the scene and put his gun away.

"Calm down," he told her. "I ain't gon' hurt you."

He showed her his hands were empty. That quieted her down, but her babies continued to cry.

"You need to shut them up," he told her. "I'm here to help you. If the laws come over here, Tristan as good as dead."

She continued to stare at him, her eyes wide. And then she did her best to comfort her children.

Her voice rattled as she told them, *"It's okay. Stop crying. It's gon' be alright."*

The toddler was obedient to his mother. He stopped crying and stared at Boom like he was the devil in the flesh. Boom thought he was right about that.

"Hey, everything alright in here?"

The voice came from the front door. All eyes moved in that direction.

Boom looked back to the woman and spoke in a hushed voice. "I know you ain't got no reason to trust me, but if I wanted you dead, you'd be dead by now. I need you to go tell that man you lost your key and had to break into your apartment. I see you scared, but try not to look like it when you talk to him."

The girl didn't budge.

"Keep acting like you don't believe me," Boom said, "and the next time you hear something about Tristan, it's gon' be somebody telling you he dead."

She got up then. She took the children with her. From the bedroom, Boom listened to the conversation.

"Hey, Pooky. Sorry about the noise. I couldn't find my key, and these babies was crying, so I kicked the door in. I'ma talk to the manager tomorrow and get it fixed."

"You kicked yo fucking door in?" The man laughed. "How the fuck you do that shit?"

Another voice, a woman's, said, "I heard a mother can lift a car to save her baby. Maybe she had some of that *mama strength*!"

"Where Tristan?" Pooky asked.

"You know that fool in the streets," the girl told him. "Hey, let me get back in here and change this diaper. I'll holler at y'all in a minute."

"What you gon' do about your door for the rest of the night?" the woman asked.

"I don't know. I'll figure something out."

Boom heard the door close, and then the lady of the house returned to the bedroom. She put the children on the bed, but they immediately whimpered and reached for her. She had to sit with them, to keep them from crying again. She looked up at Boom, her eyes as frightful as they were when he first entered.

"You did good," he said. "What's yo name?"

"Who are you?" she asked.

"I'm Boom."

Her nostrils flared. Boom wasn't sure if that meant she recognized his name.

"What's your name?" he asked again.

She told him, "Courtney."

"Alright, Courtney, I need you to call Tristan and let me talk to him."

Her eyes narrowed.

"Look," he said, "either you believe what I'm telling you; that I'm trying to save both of y'all lives, or you don't. You need to make up your mind right now."

She continued to stare at him as she dug her phone from her back pocket. She sighed and made the call.

After a moment, she brought the phone to her face and said, "It's somebody here wanna talk to you."

Tristan's voice was indignant and loud. Boom could hear it from across the room, though he couldn't make out what the man was saying.

He approached Courtney and said, "Give it here."

She handed him the phone. Tristan was still bitching at her.

Boom cut him off saying, "Say, lil' nigga, quiet down, and listen to what I'm about to tell you."

Tristan was silent for a moment before asking, "Who's this?"

"This is Boom."

Tristan didn't respond.

"Them people who was after you snatched Asha, after that shit that went down tonight," Boom told him. "I'ma try my best to get her back, but the first thing I need to do is get you somewhere safe. If they get to you, they prolly gon' do Asha right after. I figure as long as they looking for you, it'll buy me some time."

After a few beats, Tristan said, "I'm already somewhere safe."

"I'm sure you think so, but I ain't gon' feel comfortable about it unless I take you somewhere myself. I need to come get you. I'ma bring yo girl and these babies, so all y'all can be together."

"Man, I don't know about all that..."

The big man's voice boomed when he told him, "*The time for you to make decisions is done.* If you would've paid that man what you owed him, we wouldn't be in this shit. Now you got Asha caught up. Even if they don't find you tonight, yo woman and these kids gon' be dead by morning if you don't do exactly what I say. Now tell me where the fuck you at, so I can do my best to put an end to this shit."

Tristan may have been a dumbass, but he was no fool. He gave up the address. Five minutes later, Boom had Courtney, the children and two travel bags loaded in his SUV.

"I think you way smarter than yo man," Boom told her as they rolled out of the apartment complex.

"Everybody say that," Courtney replied from the back seat. "But I love that stupid motherfucker. And Lord knows these kids do. Thank you – for helping us."

"I ain't doing this for y'all," Boom said coldly. "I'm trying to save Asha. If it wasn't for her, I could care less what happens to you."

Courtney's eyes widened, and she piped down. The rest of the ride to the motel where Tristan was holed up was filled with tension and silence.

CHAPTER
21

TRISTAN DIDN'T ANSWER the door at the motel when Boom knocked. He had to return to his SUV and tell Courtney to call him. Minutes later, Tristan sheepishly emerged from the room with a backpack draped over his shoulder. He headed for Boom's headlights. He tried to get in the back, but all of the seats were filled. He reluctantly got in beside the driver.

No one talked for a while when Boom got back on the road. Tristan finally broke the silence.

"You don't think I was safe in that room?"

Boom looked up at the Motel 6 marquee in the rearview mirror before looking over at him. Tristan cowered under his hard glare.

"Do you think you were safe there?" Boom asked him.

Tristan shrugged. "Yeah, I guess so. Didn't nobody know I was there."

"Then how'd I manage to find you?"

Tristan frowned. "I told you where I was."

"You would've told somebody else," Boom predicted, "just like you told me."

Tristan shook his head. "No I wouldn't. I know how to lay low."

"What would you have done when one of Mr. Brown's men called you from Courtney's phone and said he was about to start cutting pieces off yo baby, until you told him where you were? Would you have told him then?"

Tristan grimaced. "Wouldn't nobody do nothing like that."

Boom looked him dead in his eyes. "*I would.* And I would start cutting, too."

"Could you not talk like that in front of my kids?" Courtney said from the backseat.

Boom rolled his eyes rather than respond.

"So, is it true?" Tristan asked him. "You and Asha together? She yo new partner?"

Boom looked over at him coldly before his eyes returned to the road. "Don't never ask me no question like that."

Tristan shook his head before rolling his eyes this time.

"You got a problem?" Boom asked him.

Tristan smacked his lips. "Yeah. I don't see why you gotta talk to me like that. You supposed to be helping me."

"Don't get it twisted," Boom said. "I ain't yo friend, and I ain't a nice guy. Think of every bad thing you ever heard about me." He gave him a few seconds to fill his mind with terrible things. "I'm ten times worse than all that," Boom told him.

Tristan didn't have anything else to say.

"Don't bother thanking him for taking care of us," Courtney told her man. "He doing this for Asha. He don't care if we get killed."

Tristan looked Boom's way. The big man didn't deny that. He just kept driving.

CHAPTER
22

BOOM TOOK THEM to a safehouse on the west side that he hadn't used in a while. The neighborhood was middle class, and thanks to a landscaping crew who showed up every week, even though they had never met the homeowner, the house was in perfect condition on the outside and inside. Some of Courtney's irritation and anxiety melted away when she walked in from the garage and took in her surroundings. The house was fully furnished. The appliances were mostly new, all stainless steel.

Tristan's oldest child was three years old. He must have thought his parents had finally gotten their shit together and moved them out of the hood.

"Ooh, Mama, where my room?" he squealed as he raced through the house.

Courtney tried to usher him to the living room. "Come over here and sit down, boy."

Boom redirected them. "Take them to one of the bedrooms back there. I need to holler at Tristan, before I leave."

Courtney did as she was told.

When the two men were alone in the front room, Boom asked him, "What kind of stuff you think y'all gon' need for the next few days? The freezer is stocked, but ain't nothing in the fridge. I never expected kids to be here, so I don't got no cookies or chips, or no shit like that."

"They don't need all that," Tristan told him, "just some Enfamil and diapers for the baby. She wear size one."

"Yo girl brought half a pack of diapers from the apartment. That should be enough to last a few days, but I'll bring some stuff when I see y'all tomorrow. Where yo phone at?"

Tristan pulled it from his pocket.

"Lemme see it." Boom took the phone and called one of his throwaways before handing it back to him. "You can call me on that number if it's an emergency, but don't be calling me for no bullshit. Don't tell nobody where you at. And you know you can't leave right?"

Tristan nodded. "We ain't got no car over here."

"Don't even go outside to get some fresh air," Boom said. He relented and told him, "I guess you can go in the backyard, but don't be hanging out out there all day. You smoke?"

Tristan looked like he didn't want to cop to that.

"Weed or squares?" Boom asked him.

"Both."

"Don't be getting high while you're here," Boom said. "I know you prolly feel like it'll calm your nerves, but you need to stay sober until I come get y'all. If shit go bad, I want you to have yo wits about you."

"Alright. You know anything about Asha? Is she alright?"

Boom shook his head. "I don't know nothing. Tell me everything you know about them niggas who was after you."

"The one I owe five G's is named Mook. That's the one who was chasing me. The other one who was in the car with him go by Trell. They usually hang out on Davis Street. You gon' try to find 'em?"

Boom didn't bother telling him both of those men were dead.

"You don't know nobody else in Mr. Brown's organization? Even if it's just their name, it's a start."

"The only other nigga I know that hang with them is Peel. I don't know if he work for Mr. Brown, but Mook be rolling with him."

"What Peel look like?"

"He short, dark skinned. His hair short. He got a nappy beard. He don't dress too flashy. I don't know what he drive."

"You know where Peel stay?"

Tristan shook his head then said, "I know you looking out for me and Courtney right now, but I feel like you gon' kill us after you find Asha."

Boom didn't respond. Tristan thought he saw death when he stared into his eyes.

"Is you?" Tristan asked.

Boom shook his head and softened his features. "You ain't too smart, are you?" Before Tristan could answer, Boom said, "Do you think I ever told somebody, '*I'm finna kill you*,' before I killed them?"

That sent a chill down the younger man's frame.

"But for the record," Boom continued, "I ain't got no reason to kill you. I don't like you. Matter of fact, I hate you for getting Asha caught up in yo shit. But that ain't no reason to kill you. That's enough reason for me to kick yo ass, but I ain't even gon' do that. If I get Asha back, she gon' be the one to put them hands on you."

Tristan frowned. Asha had vowed to kick his ass a couple of times that day, and now her man promised the same. Boom let him stew on that as he turned and left him in the living room. The dark killer disappeared through the garage door in the kitchen. A moment later, Tristan heard his SUV roar to life.

97

PART THREE
SYLVESTER AND PEEL

CHAPTER 23

"UHHNNNNNN."

"Uhnnnn."

"Uhhnnnnnnnn."

Asha was aware that the lighting had changed around her, but she couldn't manage to open her eyes or claw herself from what felt like the bottom of a soggy grave. She heard voices speaking, but they were echoey and disconnected, as if they were coming from the other side of a long tunnel. She wasn't aware that the moaning sounds ringing in her ears were actually coming from her.

"Uhhnnnnnnnn."

"Man, what the hell is wrong with her? You beat her?"

"Naw. She got banged up. She flipped her bike."

"Bitch sound like she got a concussion. How you know it ain't no brain damage?"

"She had a helmet on. You don't see no blood, do you?"

"Fool, she could still have a brain bleed. What I'm supposed to do if she start seizing and foaming out the mouth?"

"She ain't doing it now, so don't worry about it."

"How I'm not supposed to worry about it? You didn't say nothing about her being all banged up."

"Look at her. She fine."

"Bitch don't sound fine. She got some broken bones?"

"Naw – I don't think so."

"I ain't feeling this, Peel."

"Man, shut the fuck up and help me get her in the house."

"What if–"

"Nigga, we can talk about this once we get her inside. I don't want her to wake up while we moving her."

The second man sighed.

Asha felt weightless as they hoisted her from the trunk of the car. On one level she felt herself fighting mightily against her abductors. But on another level, she understood that she wasn't doing anything at all to stop them. She couldn't even get her eyelids to cooperate. Moving a hand or a whole limb was out of the question.

"*Uhhnnn...*"

Her perception of light was mostly foggy, tinted reddish brown, but she sensed the lighting change again when they got her inside the house.

"Where the basement?"

"It's over here."

"You got everything set up?"

"Yeah. Hold on, let met get the door."

"Nigga, why you ain't have the door open already? You knew I was on my way."

"I usually keep it closed."

"It don't matter if you usually keep it closed, dumb ass! You knew I was bringing the bitch, so yo bitch ass should've had it open!"

"Say, nephew, you ain't finna keep sonning me. I don't give a damn how hard you think you are. I ain't scared of you. You keep running yo mouth, you can turn around and take this ho somewhere else. I don't need this shit."

Peel smacked his lips. "Whatever nigga. Just hurry up and open the door."

Asha didn't hear the door open, but she felt her body being jostled as the men descended the stairs. She almost regained consciousness then, but the fog that enveloped her mind held on with a vicelike grip. Try as she might, she couldn't free herself from a darkness that felt akin to death.

When they reached the bottom, Peel asked, "Where we taking her?"

His uncle replied, "Hold up. Let me catch my breath."

"Catch yo breath? This bitch weigh a buck-forty. You better keep moving!"

"I done told you—"

"If you don't want me talking to you like this, you need to stop all this fucking complaining. Talking about *catch my breath*. You a old motherfucker, but you ain't *that* old!"

"Over here, on this bench."

After a few moments, Asha's body finally came to rest. The light was much brighter now, but from her perspective, it was still mostly muted.

"You got the handcuffs?" the uncle asked.

"Yeah."

Asha fought her hardest then, but the men didn't react to her struggles, so she knew she hadn't moved at all. She barely felt them affix the restraints to her wrists.

"Why this chain so long?" Peel asked.

"So she can sit up, eat – stand up if she want to."

"Why you want this bitch to stand up? You need to shorten these chains, keep this ho on her back."

"And then I gotta spoon feed her, slip a bed pan up under her ass every time she need to piss? Hell naw. You know I know what I'm doing."

"This the way you had it last time?"

"Yeah, and it worked. I didn't have no problem the whole time."

"What about her legs? You don't wanna put some more handcuffs on her ankles?"

"Naw. It'll be alright."

"And you want these cuffs in the *front*?"

"I just told you; I need her to be able to feed herself and go to the bathroom. I'ma give her a bucket."

"A'ight, Sly, but if you fuck this up, you know that's yo ass, right?"

"You brought her over here because you know I know what I'm doing. Remember that."

Asha realized she was finally regaining consciousness, because the sounds of the voices and the rustling chains seemed much closer now, almost completely in focus. She tried to fight again, but she was so very weak. The electric impulses that were supposed to travel from her brain, through her central nervous system, and tell her hands and arms to do what she wanted them to do continued to misfire. She feared she was paralyzed.

"Uhhnnn. Uhnnnnn. Stop."

"You hear that? She might have a brain bleed," Sly said.

"You ain't never seen a nigga get knocked out?" Peel asked. "They sound just like that. Hurry up and finish, before this bitch wake up. I don't want her to see my face."

Hearing that, Asha fought valiantly to open her eyes. Her efforts came up short yet again. The younger man's face may remain a mystery, but she was almost certain she had heard the other man mention his name. She couldn't concentrate enough to recall it at the moment, but she prayed it would come to her once she regained her senses.

When they were done with the restraints, Peel asked, "This bench secure?"

"Yeah. You see it's bolted to the floor. I just did that, when you said you was on yo way."

"You don't think she can rub these chains against it long enough to break 'em?"

"If she try, I'll hear it. I got ways to make her stop, if I catch her doing that."

The men were quiet for a minute. Asha sensed the younger one was walking around the bench, checking to make sure it was acceptable.

Finally he said, "A'ight. I'm finna bounce."

Asha tried again to open her eyes as they walked away. She rolled her head in their direction and was rewarded with a sharp pain between her temples that was so powerful, she couldn't even cry out. She gasped, like a fish out of water. Tears filled her eyes, and then the darkness came back tenfold.

This time, unconsciousness was soothing and merciful.

CHAPTER 24

UPSTAIRS, SLY AND Peel spoke in the kitchen. The older man was taller with fairer skin. He'd opted to shave his head, rather than go bald gracefully. He was clean-shaven with soft, hazel eyes. He was thin and uncharacteristically muscular, for a man his age.

Peel was short and stocky, with skin the color of merlot. He hadn't given up on an attempt to grow a proper beard, even though the hair on his face was sparse and mostly nappy. Despite the income he received from a variety of illicit activities, Peel never wore anything fancier than a pair of Dickies and a tee-shirt. Even his shoes, a pair of Chuck Taylor's, only cost sixty dollars.

He reached into his front pocket and came up with a fold of bills secured with a rubber band. He placed it on the countertop. Sly looked over at the money but didn't take it. His eyes returned to his nephew.

"A'ight, Unc," Peel said. "I'm out. I feel like I'm taking a chance by bringing this bitch here. I'ma trust you not to do nothing stupid."

"Stupid like what?"

"Like *raping* her, nigga. You know what the fuck I'm talking about."

"Why I'ma do something like that?"

Peel's look was incredulous. "Sylvester, you did twenty-five years for kidnapping and raping a bitch. Don't act like I don't know who you are."

"That's who I *was*. I changed a lot since then."

"You ain't changed that much," Peel said with a roll of his eyes. "I tell you I'm bringing a bitch over here, and thirty minutes later you got the whole scene set up and everything planned out, bolting shit to the floor..."

"That's why you brought her, 'cause you know I know how to take care of this."

"*And* you the only nigga I know who got a basement. And you live alone. You perfect for this job. I ain't gon' lie and say you ain't. Just make sure you don't hurt the bitch. You can't rape her, and you definitely can't kill her. If you fuck this up, Mr. Brown will make it easy and put a bullet in yo head. But if that ho's man find out about you, he gon' keep you alive for a week, burning and cutting skin off you. He'll make sure you feel pain in every place yo body can feel it."

If Sylvester was bothered by that, he didn't show it. "How long you want me to keep her?"

"Shouldn't be more than a few days. I'ma check with you every day, to make sure she alright. But it's some shit going down, so don't be surprised if you don't hear from me. I'll tell you this, though: If you don't hear from me for more than *three* days, that prolly mean I'm dead. You can do whatever you want to the bitch then."

Sylvester frowned. "Somebody trying to kill you?"

Peel shrugged. "You know how my work is. Nigga can die any day. But right now, it look like a war might pop off. I'ma be careful, but I might get murked. Don't nobody know how this shit gon' go."

"Sounds like what I'm doing is worth more than ten G's..."

"Nigga, you gon' get what we agreed on. I'ma bring you the other five when I come pick her up."

Sylvester stood his ground. "You need to bring *ten* more, instead of five. When we made this deal, you didn't say nothing about her being banged up, maybe with a brain bleed. And you didn't say she was all that important. That changes things."

Peel kicked himself for running his mouth. "I'll talk to my people," he said with a sneer, "see if they okay with that. I'll let you know."

He headed for the door and then turned and looked his uncle in the eyes. He told him, "Sly, I need to hear out of your mouth that you ain't gon rape her."

Sylvester's nostrils flared, but he consented. "I ain't gon' rape her."

"Put that on something." Peel knew his uncle wasn't affiliated with any street gang, so he told him, "Put it on yo mama."

Sylvester's mother had passed, so Peel knew he'd take the vow seriously.

"I put it on my mama," Sylvester said. "I ain't gon rape her. Just make sure you see about getting me that other ten."

"I told you I'll talk to 'em," Peel said before turning again and exiting the house.

CHAPTER 25

WHEN HE GOT back on the road, he called Head Buster – better known as HB. Though he'd been working in Mr. Brown's organization for over five years, Peel had yet to meet or even speak to the boss personally. He aspired to one day be as close to Mr. Brown as HB was.

HB answered after a few rings. "You take care of that?"

"Yeah," Peel said. "This a good line?"

"You free to talk."

"I don't think she hurt too bad," Peel reported, "but she was doing a lot of moaning; you know how niggas be sounding when they get slumped, and they just waking up."

"She ain't have no broken bones?" HB asked.

"Nah, I don't think so."

"You got her in a good place? You sure she ain't gon' get away?"

"She good. I got somebody watching her. Nigga I left her with done did something like this before. He know how to keep a bitch."

"Don't tell nobody where she at," HB told him. "I don't even wanna know. After the shit that went down tonight, it's some niggas in our organization who wanna get at her. It's only a few of us know you the one who took her somewhere. But if word get out, they might come at you strong, trying to figure out where she at. Let me know if somebody try to charge you up, and I'll take care of it."

"A'ight. But why we ain't killing her, though? If Fizz die, that's three niggas she done killed."

"Fizz gone," HB reported.

Peel didn't respond to that news. He meant what he said to his uncle: In their lifestyle, you could die any day.

"And we ain't killing her," HB continued, "'cause we gotta take care of a couple things first. We gon' wet her cousin and try to get Boom for a mil'. After he pay, we gon' do him and then her."

"We can do her right now and still get a mil' from him."

"What if he wanna hear her voice, make sure she still alive before he pay?"

"Oh, I didn't think about that."

"I know you didn't," HB said. "I'm tryna turn you into a boss, but you still got a street nigga mentality. You coming along, though. This shit you doing right now is *major*. You finna get blessed, all the way from the top. The boss man finally know yo name. Ain't that what you always wanted?"

Peel grinned in the darkness of his car. "Yeah, that's what I want. I'm tryna be up there with you."

"Slow yo roll," HB said with a chuckle. "Just keep playing yo part for now. Loyalty is most important, but we also gotta see you getting smarter."

"A'ight," Peel said. "I ain't gon' let y'all down."

"I know you ain't."

"Oh, one more thing; the dude I got watching her, he want ten more when I pick her up, instead of five."

"Why he change the price?"

Peel didn't want HB to know he had upped the price himself by talking so much, so he told him, "You know niggas is sheisty."

"When you go back and do her, you prolly gon' have to do that nigga too," HB said. "You okay with that?"

Loyalty for Mr. Brown quickly overrode any loyalty Peel had for his blood relative. He said, "Yeah, I'm cool with that."

"A'ight, I'll holler at you later," HB said and disconnected.

CHAPTER 26

PEEL WAS STILL beaming over his newfound acclaim when he arrived at his baby-mama's apartment ten minutes later. Unfortunately, he found that his name wasn't only ringing in circles he was comfortable with. The moment he stepped out of his car, he heard a voice behind him.

"Ay, yo, Peel."

His fight or flight response immediately kicked in. Few people knew he sometimes crashed here, and he didn't see anyone standing in the parking lot when he arrived. He couldn't believe he'd been creeped on so easily, especially after his whole crew had been warned to be on high alert. If he wasn't so distracted by his rise in Mr. Brown's organization, he would've been more cautious.

He turned slowly. If it was time to meet his maker, he would look the devil's henchman in the eyes.

He didn't express any fear when he was face-to-face with the bearded ghoul. Boom had a double-barrel shotgun trained on him. He held it at his waist, ready to fire.

Boom grunted, and Peel did know fear then. It was easier to accept the *possibility* of death, rather than look death in his eyes. He had always hoped he wouldn't see it coming.

He raised a hand.

"Wait, don't you want yo gir–"

Boom cut him off with a blast of dragon breath, giving him both barrels.

BOOM!

He didn't want to delay the identification of the corpse, so he stepped closer to the downed man and hit him again in the chest, rather than the face.

BOOM!

A second later, Boom had become one with the night. Thirty seconds after that, he was on the move, driving the speed limit, checking his surroundings. He had told Mr. Brown tomorrow would be bloody if he didn't get Asha back. He had no regrets about striking the first blow a day early.

Well, it was after midnight, so technically he'd kept his word.

CHAPTER
27

SYLVESTER DID NOT immediately return to Asha when his nephew left. He took a shower first and got himself presentable. He dressed in canvas shorts with a golf shirt. He shaved and went to the kitchen to prepare a meal for his guest. He doubted if she'd have an appetite or be inclined to eat, even if she was hungry, but he felt it would be impolite if he didn't offer.

He descended the stairs with her plate in hand. He found his prisoner awake. She sat up on the workbench with her legs dangling over the side. She watched him with an intensity that would've chilled the heart of most men, but Sylvester was casual as he approached her. It had been a quarter century since he'd seen that look in a woman's eyes, but he hadn't forgotten it. He knew exactly what she was thinking.

"Hey," he said. "I see you're awake. How you doing?"

He stopped twenty feet away and placed her dinner on an old washing machine he planned to take apart and try to fix one day.

Asha's eyes were low, but she took in every detail of his appearance and demeanor. The fact that he was okay with her seeing his face spoke volumes. She would never do such a thing, unless she planned to execute the witness.

Since she'd regained consciousness, she'd had time to take in her surroundings and contemplate her escape. She knew she was in the basement of an older house. There were two windows near the ceiling that were probably ground level. She doubted if she'd be able see anything other than grass when the sun was out – but the windows had been painted over, so she wouldn't even see that.

Her wrists were bound by a set of handcuffs. There was a heavy, coil chain attached to the middle of the cuffs, secured with a padlock. Another padlock connected the bottom of the chain to one of the legs of the workbench. The bench was metal and sturdy. Her kidnapper had draped a blanket over it, but it wasn't thick enough to make her feel like she was on a mattress or even a thin mat.

The chain had enough slack to allow her to touch any part of her body as well as stand and take a couple of steps away from the bench. The rest of the basement was used as a storage. There was an assortment of items on the shelves and stacked against the walls; none of which was within reach of the workbench.

Asha had been wondering who created this makeshift dungeon. Now that she saw him, she was wary, but not necessarily impressed. She could tell the man had done time at some point in his life. He appeared to be in his mid-fifties, but he had the physique of a 30-year-old. It was possible for him to obtain his muscle tone in the free world, but his knowledge of how to imprison a kidnap victim made Asha lean towards prior experience. His calm demeanor reinforced this thinking.

She continued to watch him, rather than respond to his question.

He stepped closer and asked, "You alright?"

Her nostrils flared. "No, I ain't alright. Why you got these fucking chains on me?"

Sylvester was pleased to hear her speaking coherently. "I'll take 'em off soon," he promised. "Sorry for the inconvenience."

"You need to take 'em off *now*."

He shook his head. "Can't do that. But it won't be long. What's yo name?"

She told him, "I need to go to the hospital. *I'm hurting bad.*"

"Where you hurting?"

"*My head*," she said. "And my arm..." She reached and gingerly touched a large scrape on her forearm. "*I need help*," she cried. "*I need a doctor.*"

"Want me to get you something for your head?" he asked. "I think you got a concussion."

"You ain't got what I need in this house. I think I got a brain bleed. I need a MRI or something. If you let me go, I promise I won't say nothing about any of this."

Sylvester smiled at his new friend. She was a little disheveled, her hair messed, and she wasn't doing a very good job of appearing to be distressed rather than furious. Beyond that, Sylvester thought she was beautiful; slim and fair-skinned with pretty pink lips and nice tits. He could tell she was cunning, but so far, he considered her manipulative skills subpar. She'd have to do a lot better, if she wanted to pull one over on him.

He told her, "You think you got a brain bleed, huh?"

She nodded and then grimaced and reached to grab her head. "*Fuck*," she moaned. "*It hurts!*"

He shook his head. "That's really amateurish."

"*What?*" she breathed.

"What else did you hear?"

She shook her head and grimaced again. Through squinted eyes she told him, "I don't know what you talking about."

"I said I thought you had a brain bleed, and now you *miraculously* diagnose yourself with the same thing..."

Asha continued to frown. She stuck to her story. "I didn't hear you say that. Just let me go, man. *I need a doctor.*"

Sylvester gave her a bored sigh. "Alright, sweetie. Well, you're not going to the hospital, so you can drop that. You ain't got no brain bleed. You got a concussion. I'm sure it's a bad one. For that, all you're gonna get is some Tylenol. I got the 500 milligram tablets, so they should help. I'll be back in a second..."

Asha maintained her position while he was gone. When the man named *Sly* returned, he had a bottle of Tylenol in one hand and a Styrofoam cup in the other. He smiled as he walked towards her. Asha couldn't believe he was going to simply hand it to her. When he was close enough, she made her move. With her teeth bared, she lunged like a dog on a leash – and much like a chained dog, her forward progress was cut short when the chain went taut. Her momentum sent her crashing to the floor. A startled "*Oomph!*" forced its way from her lungs when her shoulder impacted the concrete.

She only thought she had a headache before. Now it felt like cymbals were crashing against her brain from both sides. She was momentarily blinded by the pain and the ringing in her ears.

"*Shit!*" she grunted. She grabbed hold of her head, for real this time, as she rolled on the floor.

Above her, she heard laughter. She looked up and saw that Sly had not moved an inch. He didn't spill one drop of water from his Styrofoam cup.

"*Pah-thetic!*" he teased. He bent and placed the cup on the floor. He opened the bottle of Tylenol and bent again. He left two pills next to the cup.

Asha had made it to her hands and knees. "*Sonofabitch*," she panted hoarsely.

Her head swam, but she was able to make out something else on the floor. She hadn't noticed before, but there was a blue chalk line drawn on it. It appeared to be fresh. Sly had placed her provisions just beyond it. He was also safely on the other side.

"Since you wanna be slick," he told her, "you gotta work for these pills and that water. You can't reach it with your hands, but you can reach it with your feet, if you stretch out. Can you get the cup to your side of the line without spilling it? It would be fun to watch, but I'll leave you to it.

"And since you wanna be sneaky, you don't get dinner tonight. You don't get that bucket, either," he said, gesturing towards a large paint bucket that was close to the workbench but still on the wrong side of the line on the floor. "I hope you don't gotta go to the bathroom, 'cause you gotta hold it 'til morning – or you can piss on yourself."

"*Fuck you*," Asha growled, still on her knees, as dangerous as a trapped panther.

"I know you think you tough," Sly said as he backed away, "but you not in your world anymore. You in mine." His face became expressionless when he added, "And in my world, *bitches mind.* Hate me all you want, but by the time this is all said and done, *yo ass gon' mind.*"

His assuredness made the hair stand on the back of her neck. She wouldn't say she was afraid of him, but it would be foolish not to take him seriously. She wondered how many *bitches* had been in her position – *in his world.* Withholding medication was to be expected. But denying her the ability to pee – even if it was in a bucket – was psychological warfare. His goal was to make her grateful for the opportunity to relieve herself in such an undignified manner. If he could accomplish that, what other perversions did he have in mind. Asha shuddered at the thought.

True to his word, he took her dinner with him when he exited the basement. Asha didn't speak again as she watched him ascend the stairs. He did not close the basement door or turn off the lights. She wasn't sure if he left the lights on so she'd find it easier to get the pills or if this was a permanent thing; the lights would remain on the whole time she was there, until she couldn't tell nighttime from day.

After a few minutes, she decided to go for the meds. Lying on her side, she was able to bend her foot towards her shin and position the cup in the crook. Getting the water to her side of the line was much easier than expected. The pills were a different story. When she tried to slide them closer, they repeatedly moved to the right or left of her sneaker, like smoke flowing over a car in an aerodynamic chamber. Ten minutes passed before she had both pills in hand. By then, her face was slick with sweat, and her head hurt worse than it did when she first woke up.

And she had to pee.

She cursed the man named *Sly* and the other man, who Sly had referred to as *Peel*. She cursed Tristan for not paying his debt, but most of all she cursed herself for not listening to her man. She didn't want to accept that she was a damsel in distress, but Boom might be the only person who could save her from Sly's sick fantasies.

CHAPTER 28

CLANG!
CLANG!
CLANG!
"*I know you hear me!*"
When he didn't respond, Asha continue to bang her heavy chain against the leg of the workbench.
CLANG!
CLANG!
Finally she saw a shadow and then a figure descend the steps of the basement. Sly didn't look like he'd been asleep, but his shirt was a little wrinkled. She assumed he'd been lying in bed fully clothed.

He watched her as he stepped closer. He came to a stop on the other side of what was remaining of the blue line on the floor. Asha had inadvertently smeared some of the line with her foot, while acquiring her Tylenol and the Styrofoam cup. After seeing what she'd done, she wondered if she could use this to her advantage at some point.

"What the hell you want?" her abductor asked.

Asha stared at him coldly before her eyes moved to the left. "I want that bucket," she said, gesturing to it with a nod.

Sly looked that way and grinned when his eyes returned to her. "I told you you weren't getting it 'til tomorrow, since you wanted to pull that lil' move. It's only been a few hours. You already gotta go that bad?"

Asha had no idea what time it was, but she had a couple of beers with Murray before her cousin called and got her caught up in all of this. She didn't use the restroom before she left the Red Rooster, and she hadn't gone since. That could've been up to five hours ago.

"Just gimme the bucket," she said. "You playing too many fucking games."

Sylvester wasn't done toying with her. He walked to the bucket and then pushed it towards her with his foot. Once again, he left it on his side of the blue line. He looked her in the eyes.

"How about I make you get it from here – or you can tell me your name..."

Asha seethed, but she had no problem giving him an alias. The only problem was the man named Peel may have already told him who she was. She wondered if Sly would punish her again for being dishonest.

She told him, "Kiki."

The man continued to stare at her before pushing the bucket the rest of the way to her side of the line.

"Alright. There you go, Kiki. Go pee." His smile was sadistic.

Asha's bladder screamed, but she didn't move from her seated position. "You gon' stand there and watch me?" she asked with a sneer. "You some kind of pervert?"

He chuckled. "Naw, I was just kidding. I'll give you some privacy."

"I want my dinner too," she said before he walked away. She wasn't interested in eating, but she wondered if he'd be stupid enough to serve it with a fork.

"Oh, you hungry now?" He chuckled again. "I'll think about it."

He turned and left the room. Asha listened intently to his movements above her, but not too many sounds made it down to the basement. She feared he'd come down the stairs again once she pulled her pants down, but she had no way to avoid that, if that was his intent.

She sighed and slipped off the workbench. She saw that he'd removed the metal handle from the bucket. She grabbed the rim and moved it to the opposite side of the bench. She then positioned the blanket he'd provided her, so that it hung over the bench, all the way to the floor. It wasn't a perfect stall, but she could no longer see under the bench. From the other side, she'd be concealed from the waist down – even more so when she squatted over the bucket.

A minute later, her flow of urine felt as good as sex. She understood that Sly had accomplished his goal of making her grateful to pee in a bucket. It didn't matter. When she was done, she felt like a new woman; ready to plot another plan of escape. Her first attempt was a farce. She should've noticed the blue line on the floor and knew Sly was too smart to simply hand her a bottle of pills.

Next time would be different.

CHAPTER 29

SYLVESTER RETURNED THIRTY minutes later with her dinner. He brought her another cup of water as well, once again served in a Styrofoam cup. He placed the food on the broken washing machine and walked towards the bench. He noticed the way she'd draped the blanket over it but didn't comment on it.

Instead he said, "Bring the bucket over here."

Asha walked to the other side of the bench and hefted the bucket. She brought it around the bench but couldn't get it very close to him before the chains halted her progress. She placed it as close as she could to the blue line.

"Sit down, and push it over here with your feet," he instructed.

Asha followed his instructions. She stood again and watched while he retrieved the bucket. She knew she couldn't reach him if she lunged again, so she didn't try. He placed the bucket next to the washing machine and brought her food. A part of Asha rebelled against how unsanitary this process was. But she knew he wasn't going to allow her to wash her hands before eating, so there was no point in complaining about him not washing his.

When he placed the paper plate and water on the floor, Asha saw that her meal was spaghetti with a dinner roll. He'd provided her a plastic fork to eat it with. He walked away and found a broom in the corner of the room. He returned and used the stick end to push the plate the rest of the way towards her. He had to use the broom head to push the water. Asha noticed that he at least had the courtesy to push the bottom of the cup, to avoid any dust contaminating her water.

He backed away and watched her as she gathered her dinner. She placed it on the bench and then sat next to it.

When he didn't leave, she asked, "You gotta watch me eat?"

"I can't leave you with that fork," he said. "I'm sure you'll find a way to pick the lock on your handcuffs with it."

Asha had been thinking the same, ever since she saw it on the plate. She sighed and then smelled her food and tasted a small bite before she began to eat. The spaghetti was good. It reminded her that this was the first meal Boom ever made her, when he took her to one of his safehouses. The contrast between that scene and the conundrum she'd currently gotten herself into was stark and dismal.

"What do you do for a living, Kiki?"

"I work in an office," she said around bites.

"Doing what?"

"Making calls for an insurance company." This was the backstory she had prepared for her work buddy Murray, so the lie came easily.

"How did an insurance agent get herself in this situation?" Sylvester asked. "You slang dope on the side?"

She shook her head. "I don't know what you talking about."

"You didn't walk in here on your own free will," he said. "The person who brought you here, do you know who that was?"

She shook her head again.

"And you have no idea why he snatched you?"

She continued to shake her head.

"Kiki, you don't have to lie about everything. Don't you think it would be good if we got along?"

She looked up at him with a frown. "How I'm supposed to get along with somebody who kidnapped me?"

"I didn't kidnap you. I didn't bring you here."

"But you got me chained up and won't let me go. It's the same thing. If you don't plan on letting me go, we ain't got nothing else to talk about."

He shrugged. "Suit yourself."

He remained quiet while she finished eating. When she was done, Asha only took a few sips of her water. The bucket had served its purpose, but it was disgusting, and she wanted to use it as infrequently as possible.

"What I'm supposed to do with this?" She stood with the empty plate and the cup.

"Put the fork on the plate," he said.

Asha cringed inwardly. Nope, it wouldn't be that easy.

When she had everything he'd given her, he told her, "Put it on the floor."

She placed the items as close as she could to the blue line. Sylvester grabbed his broom and used the bristle end to sweep the items towards himself. The moment the broom breached her side of the line, Asha dropped to her butt and snagged it with her feet. Holding only the handle, Sylvester was either caught off guard or not strong enough to stop her from snatching it from him with her powerful leg muscles.

"*Bitch!*"

He almost lunged forward to take it back, but Asha quickly grabbed it with both hands. With a swift motion that would probably hurt like hell later, she shot to her feet and broke the broom across her knee. She was left standing with a jagged, wooden pole in both hands. She held them like swords, daring the kidnapper to take them from her.

"*Come on, motherfucker!*" She took a swipe at his face with one of the sharp pieces.

He jerked back and avoided getting a Joker smile.

"*Come on!*" Asha snarled. Her teeth were like a badger's, her eyes equally wild.

"*Gimme the fucking broom!*" Sylvester was just as enraged, but not angry or crazy enough to step into the danger zone. "*Gimme the broom, bitch!*"

"*Come get it!*" Asha screamed. "*I'ma kill yo ass!*"

"*You can't do shit from over there!*" he screamed back.

"*I bet I can get these motherfucking cuffs off!*"

Sylvester didn't doubt that if he left her alone for long enough, she could pry a piece of wood from the stick and pick the lock with it.

"Alright," he said nodding. "I got something for you..."

He turned and walked away. Asha's breaths were hard and heavy as she watched him head up the stairs and disappear. She didn't have time to work on the handcuffs before he reappeared, quickly making his way down the stairs. Asha saw that he had brought a gun, a black .38 revolver. His eyes were hard and serious when he marched towards the bench, stopping a few feet away from the blue line.

He pointed the gun at her face. Through clenched teeth, he said, "*Gimme the fucking broom.*"

"*Fuck you! Come get it!*"

"*I'm 'bout to blow yo fucking brains out!*"

"*Do it! Y'all gon' kill me anyway! Do it now!*"

He pulled the hammer back with his thumb. The click sounded monstrous in the echoey basement.

"You don't think I'll do it?"

"*Do it! I'd rather die like this than go through whatever shit you got going on!*"

A few seconds of silence passed while he contemplated his next move. Their breathing was audible. They both looked deranged. Sylvester was the first to soften his features. He lowered his weapon.

His voice was a lot calmer when he said, "You're not gon' die, Kiki. My friend is gonna come pick you up."

"*Who, Peel?*"

Sylvester didn't react to the news that she knew his nephew's name.

"Yeah," he said. "He's gon' come get you."

"*When?*"

"In a few days. I'm not gon' hurt you while you're down here, and he ain't gon' kill you when he picks you up. You'll be fine, as long as you don't try nothing stupid. Now gimme the broom."

Asha's frown remained fierce, but she lowered her voice as well. "You lying."

"I'm not lying. If he wanted you dead, he would've killed you. That's why you here, 'cause he need to keep you alive. He ain't gon' like it if I have to kill you, but if I tell him

I had to do it, he'll understand. I'll kill you, Kiki, if you don't gimme that broom," he said definitively. "You ain't gon' give me no choice. Now give it here."

Asha wasn't sure she believed all of what he said, but she did believe he would shoot her before he let her keep her weapon overnight.

"How long before he comes to get me?" she asked.

"He said it would be a few days, no more than three."

Asha was getting to the point where she was as good at detecting lies as Boom was, but she wasn't there yet. She believed the man had been honest with her, but maybe that was wishful thinking. In any event, the longer she remained alive, the better her chances of escape were. Sly was sure to slip up again, and once again, she'd be ready.

She lowered her arms. "If I have to stay here for three days, you gon' have to start treating me better."

Sylvester frowned. "I haven't done nothing to you."

That was laughable. *"You got me in fucking chains!"*

"I can't do nothing about that."

"But you can do something about the way you giving me my food and that bucket. Making me drag shit over here with my feet – that shit ain't right. All you're supposed to be doing is holding me hostage. You ain't gotta be fucking with my head."

Sylvester nodded. "Fair enough. But if you try to escape or attack me, I gotta do what I gotta do. Now gimme the broom."

It was hard to part with her only advantage, but Asha knew she had no choice. She sighed and tossed the broken pieces towards his feet. Sylvester un-cocked his gun and stuffed it in his pocket before he bent and retrieved both halves of the broom as well as her paper plate, cup and plastic fork. His hands full, he shot her a look before he turned and ascended the stairs again.

Asha remained in her position for a few minutes before she turned to the workbench and adjusted the blankets. She folded it in half longways, to allow for maximum comfort, and rolled the top into a makeshift pillow. She climbed on the bench and lie on her back, understanding this would be her bed for at least three days.

She stared at the ceiling for what felt like hours, trying to calm her nerves. Only one night without her man, and she missed him more than she had ever missed anyone or anything. She wanted to believe it was her circumstance that made her eyes fill with tears. But as the moisture rolled down her face, she knew the tears were for Boom. Somehow, some way, he had to find her.

Boom had no way of knowing a man named Peel was the key that would lead him to Sylvester, but Asha knew her man was resourceful. She prayed he would find the thug soon and put an end to this.

PART FOUR
DAY ONE

CHAPTER
30

"WAKE UP, NIGGA."

Perm knew the voice, but he didn't believe it was real. After the call he received from Boom last night, he assumed the demon had infiltrated his dreams. But as his eyes fluttered open and reality set in, he understood that the morning sun was out, and he was no longer asleep. There really was a man standing over his bed.

Perm immediately reached for his nightstand, where he kept a 9mm loaded and ready for intruders of any sorts. But Boom was not the average intruder. The gun wasn't there. Perm looked Boom's way again and sat up with a start when he saw that the bearded man had a gun trained on him. Perm realized it was actually *his* gun in Boom's hand. His heart shot up his throat and rattled like cymbals. His voice was uncharacteristically girlish when he screamed.

"Man, what the fuck?!"

Boom was expressionless, as usual. He rarely reacted to the full range of emotions he caused his victims to experience.

"Nigga, was you gon' shoot me with this?" he asked.

"*You goddamn right!*" Perm shouted. "*What the fuck you doing in my house? You ain't got no right to be here! I told you everything I know!*"

"Better get some of that bass out your voice," Boom warned.

Perm scooted further up the mattress, until his back was against the headboard. His sleepy eyes were now wide and very much awake. "What you want, Boom? The fuck you doing in my house? *This is my shit! You ain't got no right to be here!*"

Although Perm no longer used women's cosmetics to style his hair, his luscious mane was what he was best known for in the 90's, and the moniker had stuck with him. He now wore his hair short, the same length all around. His skin was medium brown. He was tall and lanky, in his late forties. Despite having a large nose and pockmarks on his cheeks, Perm was fairly handsome. He was also extremely popular.

If ever there was such a thing as a ghetto grapevine, Boom would consider Perm the switchboard operator. He'd known the man for more than two decades. Perm was one of those rare breeds of junkies who had overcome a devastating heroin addiction and transitioned to selling the poison that almost killed him. He was now a small-time dealer who had connections at every angle. Perm knew the addicts, the dealers, and he knew many of Overbrook Meadows' prostitutes, as they were his primary customers.

Perm operated a shooting gallery not far from the home Boom had broken into this morning. His customers were safe to get high there and stay for as long as they wanted. The things they would tell Perm could get half the city locked up if he was an informant. But his reputation on the streets was rock solid. Perm was a lot of horrible things, but he was no snitch. Even Boom found it difficult to extract information from him, which was why he sometimes had to resort to drastic measures.

He returned the man's pistol to the nightstand, within reach, if Perm was so inclined to go for it. Perm looked over at his weapon and maybe considered it before his eyes returned to Boom. By then, his indignation had given way to fear. Boom continued to stare at him with cold eyes that were always deadly and unforgiving. Perm swallowed hard and took a deep breath.

"Alright, Boom. What you want? I told you everything you wanted to know."

Boom nodded. "You told me what I wanted to know last night. Now I need to know some more stuff."

Perm's face nearly caved in on itself. The man was near tears. "Boom, I don't know nothing else," he whined. "I gave you the boy's address. I don't know nothing else about him."

"I want you to tell me everything you know about Mr. Brown's organization," Boom said. "And before you let your pride get you caught up in something you don't want no part of, I want you to understand that I'm not leaving here until I get what I want." He hefted a sledgehammer that Perm didn't know had been resting on the side of his bed.

"If I gotta start breaking shit to get you to talk, I ain't got no problem with that," Boom said. "And I ain't talking about none of yo cheap ass furniture. I'm talking about *bones*. I'll start with yo fingers and toes and save your head for last."

Perm's eyes grew even larger.

"Now, I know what you thinking," Boom said. "How am I gonna break your little bitty pinky toe with this big ass hammer."

Perm wasn't thinking that at all. Boom continued speaking.

"I'm as surgical with this thing as I am with a shotgun." He waited a few beats and then looked over at the gun. "Yo strap over there. You gon' reach for it?"

Perm continued to frown mightily. He shook his head. "This ain't right, Boom. You know it ain't right. After everything I done for you, you come at me like this?"

"I know it ain't right," Boom conceded. "But it is what it is. You gon' reach for that gun, or not?"

Tears filled Perm's eyes, and then he looked around the room anxiously. "Where, where my dog? What you do to my dog?"

"He a'ight," Boom told him. "He sleep."

"What you mean he sleep? *You killed my dog*?"

"I just told you the motherfucker sleep. I might have to kill 'em, though, if he wake up and come at me before I get outta here. The longer this takes, the worse it is for you and yo dog. *Now is you gon' reach for that motherfucking strap or not*?" he bellowed.

"*Naw, man! No!*" Perm squealed. "What you wanna know?"

Boom's nostrils flared as he placed the sledgehammer next to the bed. His first question was the most important: "Where Brionna?"

"*I don't know*," Perm cried. "Don't nobody know where she at. Some of Mr. Brown's people snatched her. That's all I know."

"*Who* snatched her? I want a name."

"*Don't nobody got a name!*"

"Somebody got a name."

"*Well I don't. I swear before God I don't! I ain't lying to you, Boom.*"

Boom believed him. His dark eyes didn't reveal how disappointed he was.

"I need to know who Mr. Brown's top lieutenants are," he said. "Start at the top and work your way down. I wanna know who driving Mr. Brown around all the way down to the corner boys selling dime rocks. I want names and addresses."

Perm shook his head in exasperation. "Boom, I don't know all them niggas. I know *of* 'em, some of 'em, but I don't know where they lay their head."

"I'm not leaving until I'm satisfied I know everything you know. I don't give a damn how long it takes. You need to make some coffee or something?"

The tears began to spill from Perm's eyes. Boom knew it was wrong to treat a close associate like this, but for Asha, he would burn every bridge in the country.

Perm sighed in resignation. "Alright," he said. "I'ma, I guess I do want some coffee. Is it alright if I check on my dog?"

Boom nodded. He waited for the man to get out of bed and then followed him to the kitchen.

CHAPTER 31

PERM MAY HAVE thought he didn't know much about Mr. Brown's organization, but he turned out to have a wealth of information. Mr. Brown's top lieutenants were Slim, OG Ruckus and Head Buster, who usually went by HB. According to Perm, all three men were extremely dangerous, but HB was particularly formidable because in addition to being well-armed, he had a reputation as a knockout artist.

"They call him *Head Buster* 'cause word on the streets is he ain't never lost a fight," Perm had said. "Whenever they got a problem with somebody they ain't trying to kill, they send HB. He like to whoop niggas in front of they people. He be taking niggas' manhood; talking shit while he whoopin' they ass."

Perm also knew a lot about Mr. Brown's low-level dealers, but Boom wanted to send a strong message, so he decided to start at the top. Perm didn't have addresses for any of the lieutenants, but he knew where some of Slim's and OG Ruckus' baby-mothers lived.

When he left Perm's house, Boom staked out one of Ruckus' women's apartments for the better part of the day before deciding Ruckus may not have a close relationship with her or his child.

He drove deeper into the hood and surveilled a few of Mr. Brown's dope spots instead. He saw enough to let him know the dealers were on high alert, leery of an ambush. Rather than peddle their product on the corner, the dope boys had employed junkies to stand there instead. The junkies directed foot traffic to alternate locations.

Boom followed them to a dozen or so newly established dope houses. The dealers rarely exited the locations. When they did, they were four deep, all armed to the teeth. They checked their surroundings before entering their vehicles and were even more vigilant when they were on the road.

But they never saw Boom.

He finally spotted his first target at six p.m. Once again, Perm's intel was on point. OG Ruckus drove a pristine white, big body Benz. He was a big man, more overweight than brawny, and he only had one goon riding shotgun with him. Boom followed the lieutenant for over an hour, long enough to know he was making pickups at some of the dope houses. Boom could've been wrong, but he suspected the boss would make the same pickups later that night or early morning.

His plan set, Boom stopped tailing the lieutenant and headed for Walmart. He hadn't slept in over 30 hours. His body yearned for rest, but before he could take care of his own needs, he had a family to look after.

CHAPTER 32

HE ARRIVED AT his west side safe house an hour later with half a dozen grocery bags in the trunk of his car. He went inside and told Tristan to go and get them. The family seemed to be getting along just fine. Courtney was in the kitchen cleaning up after dinner. The kids were in the living room, making as much noise as possible while they watched an animated movie.

Courtney was clearly uncomfortable with Boom's presence. She was courteous but quickly excused herself when she realized the large man was not going to leave the kitchen.

"I'll, uh, I'll come back and finish up in here later. We, um, we been keeping the house clean for you."

Boom nodded but otherwise didn't respond.

She left the room as Tristan entered from the garage.

"I got the diapers and Enfamil," Boom told him. "Got 'em some clothes too, but it might not be the right sizes. And I know you said they don't need no snacks, but kids want that shit, and they should have it."

"Thanks," Tristan said, not realizing Boom was taking a dig at his parenting skills.

"You heard anything?" the killer asked.

Tristan turned to face him. "I heard some of them people dead – the ones who was chasing me and two more niggas." Tristan suspected Boom had a hand in the last two murders but didn't dare ask.

"You hear anything about Asha?"

Tristan shook his head. "Naw. Don't nobody know nothing. I thought you was gon' find her."

"I'm trying."

"If we haven't heard nothing, that mean she still alive, don't it?"

Boom took a deep breath. Tristan hadn't said anything offensive, but the longer Boom remained in his presence, the more he wanted to strangle the shit out of him. Regardless of how this ended, he suspected he'd always hate this man. If it turned out Asha was dead, he'd probably kill Tristan himself, before Mr. Brown could get to him.

"I don't know if that's what it means," he said. "I'm 'bout to go. Is it something else you need?"

"Um, we, um…"

Boom clenched his teeth. Tristan had no idea that the longer he kept the monster there, the more likely someone would get hurt.

Or maybe he did understand.

Rather than finish his sentence, he said, "Naw, we good. We got enough to last us a week – or whenever it's okay to leave here."

Boom nodded. "If you hear something about Asha or anything else you think might help me find her–"

"I'll call you," Tristan interrupted. "That's all I want, is to get my cousin back. I appreciate everything you doing to help."

Boom stared at him for a second before nodding again. "Alright. I'll holler at you later."

He turned and headed for the garage door.

Tristan breathed a sigh of relief the moment he was gone.

CHAPTER 33

ASHA DIDN'T GIVE her captor any trouble that day when he delivered her meals or took her sanitation bucket away and brought it back later. Overall, she felt her confinement was horrible, but after spending seven years in prison, it wasn't something that would mentally break her. The worst part was the handcuffs and chains. The lack of ability to move very far from the workbench was something she could never get used to.

She also didn't like that Sly kept the basement lights on the whole time. Knowing what time it was was something people took for granted. Asha had to rely on her food schedule to get a general idea of where the sun was in the sky. She'd asked Sly what time it was when he brought her breakfast, but he took his watch off when he delivered her next two meals and told her he didn't know the time. Asha knew this was part of his desire to control her, so she didn't let on how irritating it was.

She didn't really like to speak to the man holding her hostage, but at the same time, it was the only thing that made her feel like she wasn't in solitary confinement. She found that Sly was very interested in conversating with her. He questioned her constantly, trying to find out why she was on Peel's shit list. Asha wasn't sure if he truly didn't know, or if he wanted to hear her side of the story. Either way, she decided it was best to continue to play dumb.

During dinner, she asked him, "What's up with you and Peel? Y'all don't seem like the kind of guys that would be friends."

"Why you say that?"

"He a thug, and you don't seem like one." Asha had no idea if Peel was really a thug until Sly confirmed it.

"I never really hung out with him, or nothing like that. But I've been knowing him a long time. We're more associates than friends."

"Why he trust you for something like this?" Asha wondered. "Out of all the people he could've asked to hold me hostage, why he pick you?"

Sly gave her a look that turned her stomach. He had always given her creeper vibes but none as strong as the one she felt at that moment. It was as if something fundamental had shifted in him. Before she asked the question, he was normal. But then for a brief moment, the beast he'd been trying to hide from her made its way to the surface. What Asha saw made her eyes widened. She stopped eating in mid bite.

And then, just as suddenly, it was gone. He smiled.

"To be honest, he said he asked me because I'm the only person he knows who got a basement – and because I live alone."

Asha continued to stare at him, wondering if he was even aware of what had just happened. Were his demons so powerful they had the ability to take control without him knowing.

"I, uh, I think I'm full," she said.

He frowned. "You sure? You won't get no more food until morning."

"Yeah, I'm good," she said, her heart stammering.

"Okay."

They went through the usual routine of him collecting her dishes, and he left her alone. Asha usually lie down on the bench after dinner, but that night she remained sitting for over an hour, staring at nothing, her mind racing.

Upstairs, Sylvester made another call to his nephew. This was his third time today. Once again, there was no answer. Peel had warned that he might not be available every day, but he also said he'd check in with him every day to make sure Kiki was alright.

Sylvester didn't know what to make of it. What he knew for sure was day one had passed, and his nephew had two more days to contact him and let him know what the next step was. Peel had said he didn't care what happened to Kiki after day three. She had seen Sylvester's face, so there was no way he could simply let her go.

CHAPTER 34

BOOM WAS ABLE to squeeze in a short nap before leaving the house at midnight wearing all black. He sported his infamous beard and ballcap. He expected his task to be daunting, so he brought a ton of weaponry and ammunition.

Thirty minutes later, he began his hunt at one of the dope houses OG Ruckus had visited earlier that day. The place was jumping. From down the block, Boom watched a steady stream of customers approach the residence. Some headed straight to a window on the side of the house. Others knocked on the door and were directed to the window. Either way, the transactions were quick and efficient.

Boom watched for more than two hours before his target finally rounded the corner and pulled to a stop in front of the house. Boom sat up in his seat, his eyes narrowed, his heart thumping with a taste for war.

From that distance, he wasn't positive OG Ruckus was in the Benz, but the fat man had been driving it earlier that day, so he had no reason to believe otherwise. The driver did not exit the vehicle at this location. Instead, the passenger door opened, and a thug emerged with an assault rifle in full view.

    The man checked his surroundings before hurrying towards the house. He went around the side and disappeared in the back. A minute later, he returned with a duffle bag in one hand, his weapon in the other. He hopped back in the Benz, and the driver pulled away from the curb. Boom gave them a head start before he started his car and began to follow them.

CHAPTER
35

OG RUCKUS MADE several pickups that were similar to the first, before he headed for the east side. At his last stop, he pulled into the driveway of a one-story home, and the garage door rolled open for him. Boom was curious as he watched him. This home was not like the ones they visited earlier. He grinned, hoping Ruckus had led him to the place where he lay his head. It was after 3 a.m., so it was likely his work was done for the day.

From down the street, Boom watched the house for an hour and confirmed no addicts were visiting this location. He slowly drove past the residence and saw that most of the lights were off. There was a park across the street from the house and a paved alley that ran past the back. Boom parked around the corner and crept to the park.

Concealed behind a playground set, he used a pair of infrared binoculars to gather intel on the house. What he saw made a deep frown appear on the side of his face.

It was a trap.

The house was teeming with glowing figures. From his vantage point, Boom counted at least five men, some posted up near the door, another peering through the front window. Everyone in the house was awake and active. Boom doubted OG Ruckus had spotted him as he followed him tonight, but he couldn't rule it out. Or maybe it was Perm who had given them a heads up.

It was ludicrous to think he could take on five men who were ready and waiting. It was equally ridiculous for Ruckus to think this show of force would deter the bearded monster from finding his woman and exacting revenge on everyone associated with her disappearance.

Boom was supremely focused when he returned to his car and popped the trunk. He geared up for the battle and left the vehicle wearing a bullet proof vest and night vision goggles. He also toted a duffle bag along with his weapon of choice for this mission, an AR-15 with an extended clip.

He knew he was being watched when he approached the house on foot. His advantage was the men in the house didn't know that he knew they were watching him. That would only buy him a little time, but if he played his cards right, it would be enough.

Boom often wondered what went through his targets' minds when they saw him headed in their direction. The men in the house would see something so formidable, they might second guess their ability to defend OG Ruckus. They might call the others to the window to check out the seasoned soldier. Rather than fear, Boom hoped they'd be overconfident.

His plan and his very life depended on it.

CHAPTER 36

IT WAS GO time the moment he stepped foot onto the property.

He hurried to the side of the house, past the windows, and was provided a bit of cover when he rushed to the electric meter. He guessed the men would move to the back of the house and wait for him to try to kick in the door, rather than exit the house and bring the fight to him.

He was right.

No one confronted him as he broke into the meter and flipped the main switch, cutting power to the whole house.

Boom dug in his duffle bag as he ran to the front of the home. Once there, he tossed two flash bang grenades through the windows. They were just as loud as they were disorienting.

PAAAP!

PAAAP!

Boom threw two smoke grenades in the same windows before running to the other side of the house. Back there, he threw two more flash bangs through the windows, coupled with two more smoke grenades.

He heard the loud shouts of chaos as he approached the patio door. Even better, he heard gunshots.

"It's him!"

"Get him!"

"I can't see!"

"He over here!"

PAP!PAP!PAP!PAP!

BLAT! BLAT!

"Who shootin'?!"

"It's him! He over here!"

"I'm hit, cuz! That nigga got me!"

Boom was almost sufficed with letting them destroy each other, but he would never leave a job unless he saw with his own eyes that the target was dead. He delivered a kick to the patio door. The sound of broken glass was enormous, but it was overshadowed by the pandemonium inside the house.

He entered the home and quickly trained his gun on a figure screaming and cowering under the kitchen table. The man didn't appear to be armed. Boom decided to save him for later.

With his night vision goggles, he saw everything clearly. Everyone else was squinting and firing blindly through the smoke. This made everything more dangerous, even for Boom, but he had the clear edge.

PAP!PAP!

"Where he at?"

"Get him!"

He bodied the first man he saw in the hallway, hitting him twice in the side.

CRACK!CRACK!

He stepped over the body and headed for the living room. Neither of the men in that room were facing him. One was trying to exit through the front door, but in his panic, he couldn't figure out how to unlock it. Boom hit him twice in the back.

CRACK!CRACK!

The other thug was trying to open the broken window. Possibly sensing the demon was in the room with him, he looked over his shoulder. His eyes were squinted, almost fully closed.

"Who over there?!"

Boom only needed one bullet to make his face explode.

CRACK!

He turned and marched down the hallway again. His next victim was headed his way. He had a pistol aimed directly at the goblin, but he couldn't see a thing.

"Stop shooting!" the goon screamed. *"Is he here? P Lowe? Is he here? Don't nobody–"*

Boom shut him up with a squeeze of the trigger. The muzzle flash briefly illuminated the hallway and sent the man flying into the opposite wall.

CRACK!CRACK!

Boom continued to march forward.

The two bedrooms on the right were empty. In the last room on the left, he finally came face to face with his target. OG Ruckus sat on the corner of the bed, his breathing labored. One hand gripped his big belly, which was leaking blood profusely. There was a submachinegun on the mattress behind him.

Boom stepped within five feet and aimed at his melon. With all but one of Ruckus' squad dead, the house was eerily quiet now.

The OG heard him clearly when Boom asked, "*Nigga, you got one second to tell me where Brionna is.*"

The boss looked up at him but could only make out a dark, menacing shadow through the smoke. "*Fuck you, Boom,*" he breathed. "*I hope that bitch dead.*"

Boom didn't have time to make him suffer as badly as he wanted to, but he allowed himself thirty seconds to ensure Ruckus' last moments on earth were filled with agony and pain.

He adjusted his aim and kneecapped him.

CRACK!

"*Aaah! You motherfucker!*"

Ruckus grabbed his leg, which had nearly been severed, and fell off the bed.

"*You motherfucker! Aaaah!*"

Boom's next nonlethal shot was to the shoulder.

CRACK!

"*Fuck you, Boom! Goddammit! Shit!*"

With the big man rolling around so much, it was hard to get the ankle shot he wanted next, but Boom was skillful and patient.

CRACK!

Ruckus began to gasp, rather than scream this time. Boom considered how many neighbors had been alerted to the carnage by now. At least one of them would've called the police. If the response time was speedy, Boom knew he had three minutes before the first squad car arrived. He growled in disappointment and ended the boss' life with two in the chest and one in the head.

CRACK!CRACK!
CRACK!
Back in the kitchen, he saw that the first man he'd encountered hadn't moved. Thinking he might be the only one to survive the massacre, the coward remained under the table. He was quiet now. Boom knew that he'd listened to all of his cohorts die one by one.

"*Get yo bitch ass up!*" he barked.

"*Boom, please don't kill me! Please!*"

"*I'm damn sho' gon' kill you, if you don't get yo ass up!*"

"*I can't see!*"

"*Crawl towards my voice!*"

The man made his way to him on his hands and knees. When he was close enough, Boom grabbed the back of his shirt and jerked him towards the patio door, almost fully lifting him from the ground.

"*Go!*" Boom ordered. "*That way!*"

He shoved him through the jagged opening. A shard of glass scraped the side of the man's face, slicing him like a tomato from mouth to ear.

"*Aaaah!*"

Boom kicked him in the ass, sending him sprawling on the back porch.

"*Shut the fuck up and move!*"

"*Where?*" the man screamed. "*I don't know where to go!*"

Boom grabbed him by the shirt again and hoisted him to a standing position.

"*That way,*" he said, leading him out of the yard. He kept a fistful of his shirt, as he shoved him in the right direction. *"Keep moving. Faster, nigga! I'm parked over there..."*

CHAPTER 37

WHEN THEY GOT to his car, Boom incapacitated his hostage with a savage blow to the back of his head before tossing him in the backseat. He fled the scene, waiting until he was nearly twenty miles away before he exited the freeway and restrained his captive with zip ties.

By the time the man came to, nothing at all made sense to him, not even up and down. A strong breeze told him he was outside. As his eyes fluttered open, he could see the stars and Overbrook Meadows' beautiful skyline. But nothing was right about what he was seeing. It took a few moments for him to realize he was upside down and very high off the ground.

Shocked into alertness, the man believed he was falling. He scrambled for something to hold on to, but there was nothing in front or on either side of him. Behind him, he felt a cold, hard surface. The wall provided no grips, but that was just as well, because the man hadn't descended an inch. Gradually he came to understand that he wasn't falling – at least not yet. But he was perilously close to doing so.

He looked up, which was actually down, and wished he hadn't. He was suspended at least ten stories high. An overpowering sense of vertigo made his head spin. He screamed as the world rotated around him and tilted to and fro.

Above him, a voice told him, "You better calm down, before you break this rope. It ain't that strong to begin with."

The man's eyes were frantic as he looked down, which was actually up. He couldn't bend his neck enough to see past his own body, but he saw that he was close to the roof of a building. Both of his legs were bound at the ankles. The ropes cut into his flesh, causing him to lose all sensation in both feet. His arms were bound behind him.

"*Help me!*" he screamed. "*Please, Boom, let me up!*" Blood dripped down his face, into his eyes. He couldn't remember what had caused the wound.

"I'ma let you up," the voice called from above. "But I need you to give me some answers first."

"*I don't know where she at!*" the man cried. "*I don't know! Don't nobody know!*"

"Wrong answer."

The man heard the unmistakable sound of a switchblade opening.

SHIK!

"These knots too tight," Boom told him. "I'ma have to cut you down."

"*Nooo! Don't do it! Don't cut the rope!*"

The man fought valiantly, without a clear goal in mind. Even if he could fold his body enough to reach the rope around his legs, without his hands, he was helpless.

"I ain't got no choice but to cut," Boom said, "if you don't know where Brionna at. I'm willing to reward you with your life, but you gotta gimme something first."

"*I don't know!*" the man blubbered. "*I swear to God, I don't know!*"

From his vantage point, Boom knew he was crying.

"*Don't nobody know where she at! They won't tell nobody! Ruckus don't even know. Mr. Brown, he the only one...*"

Boom sighed. "Okay, tell me where I can find Mr. Brown."

"*Please, Boom. Please don't do this. You know I don't know where he at. I ain't never been to his house. Ruckus know, and HB, but they the only ones.*"

Boom knew the man was telling the truth. Mr. Brown wouldn't have made it this far if every member of his organization knew where he slept. It made sense that only the top members of his organization were privy to that information.

"I guess you ain't got nothing for me," he said.

A second later, the dangling man heard something that would haunt him for the rest of his short life. It was the sound of a knife cutting rope.

"*No, Boom! Pleeease! I wanna help you, but I don't know nothing!*"

The cutting stopped briefly, and then Boom said, "Next time, make sure yo dumb ass know something."

"Huh – *what?*"

The cutting started again. It was swift and to the point this time.

Boom listened to the man scream as he fell, but he felt no need to look over the side of the building and watch his descent. It was rare, but sometimes you don't have to see the corpse to know for sure the target is dead.

CHAPTER 38

BOOM WAS ON the freeway, almost all the way home when he received a call. Only three people had reached out to him on this particular cellphone in the past month. One of those men was Perm. The other was the dangerous Mr. Brown. Boom had memorized the kingpin's number. He wasn't surprised to see it on the caller ID.

He answered with a bored, "Yeah."

The voice on the other end was gravelly and bass-filled. "You think any of this is gon' get yo bitch back?"

The fact that Mr. Brown had made the call himself and was unable to hide his frustration told Boom all he needed to know: He was winning.

"I told you," he replied, "if I didn't get her back, all yo soldiers going down, one by one. I'm just one man, though, right? So this might take a while."

Mr. Brown fumed. Boom savored the sound of the crime lord's sigh.

"I'ma tell you something," Mr. Brown said, "I warned you not to let yo hot head get you in something. And just like

I figured, you only made things worse for yourself. I don't want yo bitch. I told you I was gon' give her back."

"Yeah, after you taxed me and taught her a lesson. I told you that was a no-go."

"And I told you you don't get to decide."

"I'm deciding what's happening now, though, ain't I? And I'ma keep deciding, 'til you turn her loose. You think I'ma stop before I get her back? Thangs gon' get even worse, if she ain't alright."

"What I think is this shit ain't worth my time."

"Turn her loose then."

"Boom, I'ma tell you something yo ass prolly ain't gon' believe: Only one of my people knew where yo gal was. I told the nigga not to tell nobody, 'cause I wanted to keep her safe. That nigga just happened to be the first one you went after."

Boom's body froze. He almost had to pull off the freeway to process what he'd just heard. He managed to keep his voice neutral when he asked, "Who the fuck you talking about?"

"I'm talking 'bout *Peel*. Did you even ask that nigga about yo gal, before shit went sour?"

Boom's mind quickly took him back to the fatal moment.

Ay, yo, Peel.

Wait, don't you want yo gir–

BOOM!

Without seeing Mr. Brown face-to-face, Boom couldn't be confident the kingpin wasn't lying to him. But the possibility that he was telling the truth was devastating.

"How only one nigga know where she at?" he asked.

"I'm telling you I didn't want nobody on my side going after her, after what she did that night. If none of us knew where she was, couldn't nothing happen to her. Plus I didn't want you to hem up one of them niggas, and they start running they mouth."

"You telling me Peel didn't even tell you?"

"I didn't get a chance to talk to him. Nigga was gone by morning."

Boom was torn between wanting to believe Asha was still alive and thinking Mr. Brown was trying to trick him. So far, all the evidence pointed to this being the truth. Perm had told him no one knew where Asha was. OG Ruckus said he *hoped* Asha was dead, rather than indicate definitively whether she was or not. He was a top lieutenant in Mr. Brown's organization, so wouldn't he know for sure? Even Boom's last victim took a ten-story freefall rather than say where Asha was.

Boom may not have all the answers, but he did know where this conversation was headed.

"I need you to back down," the boss said. "Gimme a minute to try to find yo woman. It'll be easier for me to do that without all this killing going on."

"Let you tell it, she gon' die either way," Boom replied gruffly. "Yo man put her somewhere, and ain't nobody looking after her."

"Peel had somebody looking after her," Mr. Brown countered. "But don't nobody know who that is."

"You full of shit."

"Believe what you want. But I'll tell you this: If you don't stand down, I ain't gon' waste my time looking for the ho. I'll put all my efforts into dealing with you. If you give me some time, I'll try to find her. What happens next is on you."

The line went dead. Boom placed the phone on the passenger seat and drove the rest of the way home in silence. He couldn't stop his mind from racing, imagining Asha in all sorts of dark, precarious situations. Even if Mr. Brown was telling the truth about someone looking after her, that thought was not comforting. Her captor could range anywhere from a comforter to a sadist.

Boom hadn't cried in decades, but the freeway suddenly blurred. He had to wipe the moisture from his eyes to avoid drifting towards the median and crashing into a guardrail.

Once his eyes were dry, they quickly reddened. His body heated, and he welcomed the new emotion. Rage had always been a better companion.

PART FIVE
DAY TWO

CHAPTER 39

ASHA DIDN'T SLEEP well after her first full day in Sly's dungeon. She felt like every time she closed her eyes, she got a vision of the look on his face when she asked why Peel had selected him as the person who should hold her hostage. She already knew her captor had sadistic tendencies. She now wondered how deep his debauchery truly was.

At lunchtime on her second day, she engaged him in conversation more aggressively than she usually did. She desperately needed to know that the man she was forced to spend time with was somewhat *normal*.

"How come you haven't been to work since I got here? You got a job?" she asked while she ate two chicken drumsticks with a side of corn.

The one thing Asha was chagrined to admit that she didn't hate about her time in the basement was the food. Sly could've given her a dry ham sandwich at every meal, but he always took the time to cook something, even for breakfast. Asha considered his cooking above average. She wondered if he'd honed his culinary skills in prison or throughout his life as a bachelor.

In response to her question, he said, "I took off work for the next few days. I didn't wanna leave you here by yourself. I'm sure you'd find some sort of mischief to get into, if I leave you alone."

Asha rolled her eyes. He was right about that.

"What you do for a living?" she asked.

"Why you wanna know?" He sat across from her in a metal folding chair. He had taken to bringing the chair with him during mealtimes, rather than stand and watch her eat.

She told him, "I'm just curious."

"What insurance company you work for?" he asked in return.

"What I'ma tell you that for, so you can try to find me when I get outta here?"

"No, *I was just curious*," he teased.

Asha wasn't willing to give in to his quid pro quo, so she switched gears. "Why you live here by yourself?"

"I'm not always by myself. Women come, and women go."

"You had women living here with you?"

He nodded.

"What you do to scare them off?"

He grinned. "Why you think I scared them off?"

"Maybe they found out you're holding women hostage down here..."

His eyes narrowed, and then he smiled.

"That's it, ain't it," Asha said. "Don't nobody wanna be with you, once they find out what kind of freak you are."

"Maybe the women I've been with are the ones with problems, and I kick *them* to the curb."

"Yeah, let you tell it."

"Why you attacking me? I ain't do nothing but bring you lunch."

"Fool, you got me locked up, and you won't let me go. I ain't finna give you no credit for feeding me. That's the least you can do."

"Fine. But why you got this attitude today? I do something to make you mad – *other* than not letting you go."

Asha sighed. "I need to brush my teeth. And I wanna take a bath."

Sly grinned.

"That's that creepy shit I'm talking 'bout," she snapped. "You know how hard it was for me to tell you that?"

"Okay, I'm sorry." His smile went away. "But you know I can't let you out of here."

"You can bring me a clean bucket and some water and soap and a washcloth – something to dry off with too."

Sly wondered why she was willing to take a monkey bath in a bucket, rather than demand he take her to a tub, but he didn't question it. Kiki appeared high maintenance, but she was clearly accustomed to the rough side of life.

He said, "Okay, I can do that."

"You got a new toothbrush?"

"I got a toothbrush I ain't used yet."

She shook her head. "If it ain't still in the wrapper, I don't want it. Just bring me some mouthwash."

"Alright. You want that now, or..."

"Let me finish eating first."

He nodded. "Okay."

When she was done, and he'd collected her dishes, Sly went upstairs and came back with the mouthwash. Asha didn't like that the bottle of Listerine was open and half full, but she didn't plan on swallowing it, so she figured it was okay. Besides, she'd been eating and drinking everything he brought down there. If he wanted to poison her, he could've done it by now.

He poured the mouthwash in a Styrofoam cup and told her to go to the opposite side of the workbench, while he placed it past the line on the floor. When he was done, she retrieved the cup and rinsed her mouth for the first time in two days. She spat in the cup and left it on the floor for him.

Sly had several empty buckets in the basement. He took one of them upstairs and was gone for ten minutes. When he returned, Asha saw that he'd removed the metal handle. She could tell by the way he toted the bucket, that it was half filled with water. Again, he told Asha to walk to the opposite side of the bench before he placed it on her side of the line.

He'd taken to doing this a lot lately; asking her to move, rather than pushing items over with a broom. Asha wondered if she could reach him in time, if she hopped over the bench or tried to run around it. She was doubtful. Sly only had to take a step back to avoid her. He was sure to punish her by withholding a meal or her sanitation bucket, if her attack was unsuccessful.

He went upstairs again and came back with the towels and soap she'd requested. Thankfully the bar of soap was still in the box unopened. This time he remained on his side of the line and offered to toss the items to her.

"You can catch, right?"

"Yeah, 'preciate it."

When she had everything she needed, he hesitated, his eyes narrowing.

"What?" she asked him.

"Go ahead and open that soap and gimme the box back," he told her.

"You think I'ma pick my locks with a piece of cardboard?"

"I can't put nothing past you. If you want me to leave you alone, so you can bathe, gimme the box. Otherwise I gotta watch you."

Again, Asha was struck with the notion that he was too comfortable with the role he was playing. She knew that whether she gave him the box or not, he *wanted* to watch her. He'd probably try to creep down the stairs while she was distracted.

She opened the soap and tossed the box back to him. Before he left, she asked, "Can you close the door up there, so I'll know when you trying to come back down. I may not be done."

He shook his head. "Can't do that. I need to hear if you scraping them chains, trying to break 'em off. Besides, if I open that door *real quiet like*, you wouldn't be able to hear it no way."

As he stared at her, Asha saw the monster break through to the surface again. The change in his eyes was both subtle and drastic at the same time, like a pit bull that goes from sniffing your hand to trying to rip it off in a matter of seconds. And then, just as quickly, the demon was gone.

"But I ain't got no reason to sneak down here while you bathing," he said. "I ain't no pervert, like you think I am."

He turned and left her alone. Asha watched him go and waited, not believing a word he'd said.

After five minutes, she set up her bench with the blanket draped over it, like she usually did when she used her sanitation bucket. She took the water to the safe side of the bench and kept her eyes on the basement stairs as she removed her shirt and bra. She remained squatted as best she could, just in case the creep tried to sneak up on her. She washed her face, neck and underarms and hurriedly dried off and put her shirt back on.

She removed her sneakers, jeans and panties and cleaned her other lady parts before pulling the jeans back on without the panties. When she was done getting dressed, she debated what she should do with her bra and panties. After two days, the bra had become uncomfortable, especially while sleeping. And putting her dirty panties back on would defeat the purpose of the bath. Asking Sly to discard her unmentionables was out of the question. The freak was sure to take them upstairs and sniff them for hours, if not days.

She looked around the basement as she balled the undergarments into a tight wad. In the corner of the room on her side was an old bookshelf that wasn't flush against the wall. If she threw high and hard enough, she could get her underwear over and behind the bookshelf. Sly would never know they were there.

She gave it a shot and *almost* made it. The underwear made it to the top of the bookshelf, but they didn't fall over the back. Asha could see them sitting atop the furniture. Hopefully that was because she knew where to look. She doubted if Sly would randomly spot them when he returned.

Upstairs in his bathroom, Sylvester watched everything on two hidden cameras he had installed in the basement. The first camera faced the front of the bench, so it only captured glimpses of Kiki's breasts while she cleaned herself. The second camera picked up everything on what she considered the safe side of the bench.

He saw *everything*.

He was so excited, he shot his load while she rubbed the washcloth between her legs. He made a mental note of where she had tossed her underwear. He wasn't sure how he'd get them without her knowing, but he had his ways.

He didn't bother cleaning up the mess he'd made in the sink before he rewound the video on his laptop and squirted more lotion in his hand. He began stroking the moment Kiki took off her shirt. He made it all the way to the end of her bath this time. He rewound it again. This time he came while staring at her bare ass. He couldn't wait to see it in person. He salivated at the thought of spreading her cheeks and licking her asshole. He knew she'd love it.

CHAPTER 40

AROUND THE SAME time Sylvester allowed his perversions to take him to another level of depravity, Boom received a call from the man at the top of his shit list. He hadn't decided if he was going to kill more of Mr. Brown's men that night. He suspected this conversation would be the deciding factor.

He didn't attempt to hide his annoyance when he answered. "What, nigga?"

"You got a hard time showing respect," the crime boss noticed.

"I respect your reputation," Boom told him, "But I ain't got no respect for the circus show you got going on over there. You supposed to be the boss. I wanna give you the benefit of the doubt, but I got a hard time believing you don't know where my girl at."

"I know you do, that's why I'm offering a concession."

Boom frowned. *"A concession?"*

"Yeah. I'm willing to let you work with me to try to find her."

Boom smacked his lips. "How that shit gon' work?"

"I'ma send you one of my men. He know all Peel's connections. He the one who was grooming him. He was already gon' spend the day looking for your gal. I think you'll believe that I'm putting some effort into this if I let you roll with 'em."

"That's the dumbest shit I ever heard," Boom replied gruffly. "You think I'ma hop in the car with some nigga who tryna kill me?"

"You tryna kill us too, but that don't mean we can't put our differences aside and try to find out where yo girl is. If I called you tonight and said I couldn't find her, you know you wouldn't believe me. But if you go with him, you can see for yourself. Hell, y'all might luck up and find the bitch."

Boom considered that and asked, "Who this nigga you talking about?"

"He go by HB."

Boom remembered everything Perm had told him about *Head Buster*. He suspected a trap, but Mr. Brown had another thing coming if he thought it would be this easy. Boom decided that if he accepted the offer, the worst thing that would happen was they wouldn't find Asha. If that turned out to be the case, he was sure to take HB's life at the end of the ride. The lieutenant was next on his list anyway.

"If I agree to this," Boom said, "he ride with *me*, not the other way around. And he gotta let me frisk him before he get in the car."

"So you get to be armed, but he don't?"

"I ain't gon' hurt the nigga, long as he don't try nothing."

After a pause, Mr. Brown said, "From what I heard, you a solid nigga, Boom. People say they can trust what you tell 'em. If we do it your way, you gotta give me your word that you ain't gon' be the one to try something. HB can take care of hisself, but not if you got a pistol and he don't…"

Boom knew that if he gave his word, it would cost him a chance to exact revenge on one of Mr. Brown's top men. So be it. If it would help find Asha, it was worth a try. He could always come back and kill HB later, along with Slim and finally Mr. Brown himself, if need be.

"I give you my word I ain't gon' kill the nigga," he said, "as long as he don't try nothing."

CHAPTER 41

THIRTY MINUTES LATER, Boom received another call on the cellphone Mr. Brown had used to reach him. This time, it was a number he didn't recognize.

He answered with a guarded, "Yeah...?"

"What up," a male voice said. "This HB. I'm supposed to be meeting you somewhere, so we can go on a ride..."

Boom wasn't sure if he'd purposely used such an ominous phrase. In their line of work, the *ride* usually ended with one of them taking a bullet to the head.

He gave him an address to a public location that wasn't too crowded. "How soon can you be there?"

"Gimme about thirty minutes..." HB replied.

CHAPTER 42

BOOM ARRIVED AT Lisa's Chicken on the north side of town ten minutes early. He waited across the street at a small strip mall. He wasn't sure what HB was driving, but he saw a silver Mustang pull into the restaurant's parking lot ten minutes later. No one exited the vehicle. Boom saw that there was only one person in the car. A minute later, he received a call from the same number HB had used earlier.

"Yeah," Boom answered.

"I'm here."

"Alright. Get out yo car," Boom said, watching the Mustang.

"Get out and go where?"

"Just get out the car for now. I'm finna tell you what to do."

Boom waited and watched. The Mustang's door swung open, and a large man exited the vehicle. Even from across the street, Boom saw that HB was a force to be reckoned with. Head Buster's arms and chest were massive. He had a thick neck that was perfect for football or boxing.

Boom was a big guy himself, but he thought HB had the advantage, when it came to size and muscle mass. Typically, a man his size had to trade speed for strength, but he knew HB was a notoriously successful streetfighter.

"A'ight, I'm out," the bruiser said. "Where you at?"

Boom had not seen any other cars following the Mustang or lurking at a distance. He was confident HB had come alone.

"Turn around," he told him. "You see this AT&T store over here?"

HB held the phone to his ear as he turned and eyed the strip mall. "Yeah, I see it."

"Cross the street and come over here."

"A'ight," HB said. He turned back to his car. "Why you ain't tell me to meet you over there in the first place?"

"Naw, I need you to walk," Boom told him.

HB turned back in his direction, but he couldn't spot the man he was supposed to be meeting. "You want me to walk across this busy ass street?"

"Yeah. I'll tell you where I'm at when you get over here."

Boom could see he wasn't happy about that, but HB followed his instructions. When he made it across the street, he looked around, still holding the phone to his ear.

"A'ight, I'm over here. Where you at?"

"Come towards the phone store."

HB walked in that direction. "Now what?"

"Turn to your right and walk this way."

HB continued to frown as he did so.

When he was close to his vehicle, Boom told him, "Alright, stop. Lift yo shirt up."

HB looked around but still hadn't spotted the black Challenger. "Nigga, you on some *other* shit," he commented.

Boom didn't respond.

When HB lifted his shirt, Boom told him, "Keep the shirt up and turn around."

HB followed these instructions as well.

Boom exited his vehicle then and walked up to him. He hung up when he was closer. He told him, "Don't turn around. Yo boss told you I had to frisk you?"

HB looked over his shoulder, and the two men locked eyes for the first time. HB saw the bearded beast who had been terrorizing his organization. Boom saw an intimidating goon who had no fear in his coal black eyes.

"You gon' let me frisk you or not?" Boom asked. "If not, you can take yo ass back to yo car and get gone."

"Hurry up, nigga."

Boom checked him for weapons. He found none.

"A'ight," he said. "I'm parked over here."

HB turned and faced him, sizing him up. "So this how the bad ass Mr. Boom done stayed alive so long..."

Boom didn't reply to that. "I'm parked over here," he repeated.

CHAPTER 43

RIDING AROUND WITH an enemy should've been nerve-racking, but Boom found HB surprisingly likable. He didn't seem to harbor any ill will about what happened last night.

"How you get *all* them niggas?" he wondered. "I know you cut off the lights and threw some smoke in that bitch..."

Boom looked over at him and frowned. "I ain't finna talk about nothing like that."

"Why? I'm just asking."

"'Cause I ain't finna incriminate myself in no shit."

HB laughed. Boom's frown grew deeper as he stared at him.

"You think I'm *police*?" HB cackled. "You should know better than that!"

"I don't know what type of shit you on."

"Yeah you do. You know what I do for a living. If it'll make you feel better, I killed a couple of niggas last week. Tommy Pearson and Jamil Robinson. You prolly saw that shit on the news. *Double homicide.* I fucked around and shot an innocent bitch too, but she gon' make it."

"What that got to do with me?"

"I'm tryna make you feel better about talking about yo shit. I just incriminated myself, so you know I ain't tryna get you caught up."

"Yeah, well, I don't care who you killed. You ain't finna get me to talk about nothing like that."

"Damn, nigga, you so careful yo ass *boring*! Well, at least tell me this: What OG Ruckus say to you, to make you fuck him up like you did?"

"Say, man, even if you ain't trying to hem me up with the laws, them still yo people. I ain't tryna piss you off, with you sitting this close to me."

"Them ain't my people," HB said. "If we ain't got the same blood, they just some niggas I work with."

Boom had a hard time believing he was that unbothered.

"At least tell me if that fat motherfucker begged for his life," HB said.

Boom shook his head. "I don't know what you talkin' 'bout."

HB rolled his eyes. "Hmph. I guess that mean you ain't gon tell me about P Lowe either."

"Who?"

"The nigga that went skydiving with no parachute."

Boom's eyes narrowed. He remained mute.

"My nigga," HB complained, "you dropped a nigga over the side of a building, and you can't tell me nothing about it? I done killed a lot of people, but I ain't never dropped nobody off a building. You don't never like talking about yo shit?"

Boom shook his head. "Hell naw."

"I swear, my G, you good at what you do, but you ain't no fun to be around. You prolly ain't got no friends."

Boom couldn't help but crack a smile then. "I can't believe you right now. Six of yo people get murked last night, and yo ass trying to make a new friend. You on some weird shit."

"I told you, them ain't my people. Only one I can say I'm gon' miss is my nigga Peel."

Boom looked over at him, thinking he'd express anger at that point, but HB simply shrugged.

"I ain't mad at you, though. We all know the rules when we play this game. Nigga can die any day."

Boom watched him for a moment longer, before his eyes returned to the road. He said, "I don't know nobody name Peel. I don't know what you talking 'bout."

CHAPTER 44

THEY GOT DOWN to the business at hand, starting first at Peel's baby-mother's apartment. It was rare for Boom to revisit one of his crime scenes, but his expression remained neutral as he entered the apartment complex. If he was uncomfortable about being there, HB couldn't tell.

Before the lieutenant got out of the car, Boom told him, "Call me on yo cellphone."

HB frowned. "Call you? Now? What for?"

"I wanna be on the phone while you in there, so I can hear what she say."

"You don't trust me to tell you when I get back?"

Boom shrugged. "Maybe you wanna call some of your people while you in there, tell 'em I'm outside waiting. I wanna hear if you do that too."

"*Daaamn!*" HB laughed. "Yo ass done thought of *everythang*! Yo, I'm feeling this shit. You a professional, Boom. Straight legit. I wish I came up under a nigga like you. Maybe when this shit all done, you can come work for us."

Boom shook his head. "Nah, I'm good. I don't like working for nobody. And just 'cause *you* ain't got a problem with me don't mean the rest of yo squad feel that way."

"Yeah, you right. But I wish we had linked up under difference circumstances. Nigga could learn a lot from you."

Boom was surprised by his candor. He hadn't known him for very long, but he felt HB was one of the most honest people he had ever met.

HB called his phone, and Boom told him, "Keep the phone in yo hand. You might accidently hang up, if you put it in yo pocket."

HB didn't protest this time. "A'ight."

He left the car, and Boom watched him mount three flights of stairs before knocking and disappearing inside one of the apartments. He listened to the conversation as he left his parking spot and repositioned himself in a fire lane three buildings down. Inside the apartment, Boom heard a woman trying to quiet a crying baby.

HB told her, "Hey, I'm sorry about what happened to Peel. You alright? You need anything?"

The woman's response was ripe with grief. "Y'all ain't found out nothing? Don't nobody know who did it?"

Boom wondered what was going through HB's mind at that moment. Not only did he know who did it, but he'd been palling around with the triggerman for the last thirty minutes.

"Nah, but I think we getting close to figuring it out," HB replied. "Here. I know it ain't much, but I hope it helps."

"It will. Thanks. I appreciate you looking out for us."

"I gotta ask you something. The night Peel got killed, did you talk to him before he came over here?"

"Just for a minute. He said he was on his way. Next thing I know, somebody told me he just got shot in the parking lot."

"Did he tell you where he was before he came here?"

"No. He usually don't be talking to me about his business."

"Are you sure he didn't say nothing? That night, I told him to hide something very important for me. He took it somewhere, right before he came over here. I really need to find it."

After a pause, the girl said, "I don't know where he was. He didn't say nothing to me about hiding something."

"Alright. Well, can you think of anywhere he might'a took it?"

"I don't know. Maybe his mama's house... He usually be with Fizz and Mook, but I heard they got killed too. If he didn't leave it with either of them, I don't know."

"Okay. If you hear something, gimme a call."

"You think it's somebody trying to take all of y'all out? You gon' be okay?"

"Yeah. I'm good. I know shit look bad, but we gon' get to the bottom of it."

"HB, if you, uh, if you ever need somewhere to chill, you can come over here. The baby don't cry that much. I really don't like being over here by myself. You, um, you know I always been liking you."

Boom's eyes widened, but he wasn't too shocked by what he was hearing. It wasn't uncommon for a hood chick to hop from one gangsta's dick to the next, even if the men were friends. But Boom thought it was a little too soon for this hoodrat to shoot her shot.

"I'll holler at you about that later," HB told her. He left the apartment but didn't see Boom's black Challenger when he got downstairs. "Where you at?" he asked, speaking into the phone. "You left me?"

"Naw. Start walking to the left," Boom told him.

"Goddamn. We doing this shit again?"

"I gotta frisk you again too," Boom informed him, "before you get back in the car."

"You think I ran in there and grabbed a gun? You was listening the whole time."

"You ain't gotta say a word to pick up a pistol and put it in yo pocket."

"A'ight, man. Whatever. Ay, you hear how that bitch was tryna throw the pussy at me?"

Boom could see HB's smile, even from a distance.

"That shit was foul as hell," HB said. "I'ma fuck her, though. You should'a seen that broad. Got some fat ass titties!"

CHAPTER 45

THEY REPEATED THE same routine at Peel's mother's house, with two of his homeboys who were not affiliated with Mr. Brown and one of his cousins. HB stopped complaining about Boom's car not being where he'd last seen it at any of these locations, and he consented to getting frisked each time he returned to the Challenger.

Boom was beginning to give up hope that they'd find Asha until they made it to the cousin's house. The woman didn't have a solid lead, but she said something they hadn't heard before.

"Why don't you check with Sly? If Peel was hiding something he didn't want nobody to know about, he might'a left it there."

"Who's Sly?" HB asked her.

"That's his crazy ass uncle. Don't nobody in the family fuck with him, but I think him and Peel was still kinda close."

"A'ight. 'Preciate your help," HB said before leaving.

When he got back to the car, he told Boom, "She didn't know nothing. I got one more person I wanna check. I forgot Peel had another bitch on the side."

"What about that uncle?" Boom asked. "You don't wanna check him out?"

"I think I heard about that nigga. He some kind of square," HB replied. "He wouldn't be keeping no bitch hostage."

"It wouldn't hurt to call him. Leave no stone unturned."

HB sighed as he reached for his phone. "I guess... But I'm telling you this ain't the one."

He called the cousin he'd just spoken to. "Say, you got a number for Sly? I wanna holler at him."

The woman said something, and HB told her, "Bet." He looked over at Boom and said, "She gon' call some people. She say she'll call me back."

Boom had nearly made it to Peel's other woman's house when HB's phone rang.

"What up, Yvette?" he answered. A few seconds later, he said, "Thanks." He looked Boom's way and said, "Got Sly's number."

"Put him on speaker," Boom instructed.

HB made the call. After a few rings, a man answered. "Hello?"

"Yo, this Sly?"

"Who wanna know?"

"My name HB. I used to work with yo nephew Peel."

After a few beats, the man on the other end said, "Okay. What's up?"

"The night Peel died," HB said, "did he come by yo house and drop something off? He was holding something very important to me. I told him to put it somewhere safe, but he didn't get a chance to tell me where he left it, before he got killed. Did you see him that night?"

"Peel dead?"

"Yeah. He got killed a couple of nights ago."

"Oh, shit, I didn't know that."

"Did you see him the day before yesterday?" HB asked.

"Naw. I haven't seen him in – damn near a year."

"A'ight. I appreciate yo help."

"Do you know who killed him?" Sly asked.

"Naw, but we working on it. I'll let you know if we find out something." HB disconnected and looked over at Boom. "I told you that nigga don't know nothing. Run me by Trivette's house. I got a good feeling about this one."

For the first time since HB had gotten in his car, Boom felt the man was being dishonest with him. His radar wasn't perfect, but Boom had a sixth sense when it came to lies. He wasn't sure if HB was lying about Sly or Trivette, but something wasn't right.

"I think we should go see that uncle," Boom said. "He sound a little squirrely to me."

"I got a good feeling about Trivette," HB repeated. "I know Peel was closer to her than his baby-mama. He tell that bitch everything. If she don't know nothing, I guess we can try to find Sly."

Again, Boom knew the man was holding something from him. He played it cool and continued to Trivette's house. "Alright," he said with a nod. "We'll check her out first."

CHAPTER 46

BOOM LISTENED TO much of the same nothing while HB was inside Trivette's house. She was more distraught than Peel's baby-mama, and she didn't know a thing. Boom moved his car down the street and went through the same process of directing HB to him and frisking him when he returned to his car.

While patting him down, Boom discovered why HB had seemed anxious. The musclebound man spun suddenly and caught Boom with a chop to the side of the head. Boom was stunned both by the unexpected violence and the force of the blow. He stumbled backwards, his head spinning. HB pressed the attack.

Perm had said HB had a habit of talking shit while he was whooping ass. That was not the case today. The big man was as serious as a stroke as he threw one power shot after another. Boom had not recovered from the first strike before he got caught again – this time in the jaw. He dodged most of a crushing right hook, but it still slipped off his nose, causing it to immediately gush blood.

Boom had always felt he could throw hands with the best of them, but HB's reputation was well earned. Boom knew he couldn't take him in a fair fight. With stars in his eyes, he put all his force into a kick to the nuts that struck pay dirt. None of HB's muscles could help him with the excruciating pain that radiated from his balls, all the way up to his chest.

He reached reflexively for his family jewels, and Boom lay into him, clobbering him with hook after hook. They all landed flush on the jaw and side of the face. After five blows, Boom feared the behemoth wouldn't go down, but he dropped him with the sixth punch.

Boom caught his breath and wiped his nose as he staggered to his car. He left a trail of blood as he grabbed a couple of zip ties from under the front seat. He returned to the downed man and bound his arms behind his back. He didn't want to take any chances, so he zip-tied his ankles too.

In all the years he'd been abducting people, HB was the heaviest man he'd ever hauled into the backseat of his car.

CHAPTER 47

HB AWAKENED IN the same building and the same chair a man named Banks had found himself in on the last night Asha and Boom were together. Rather than allow him to come to his senses on his own, Head Buster was unceremoniously jarred to consciousness with a bucket of water splashed in his face. He struggled briefly, as his mind tried to come to terms with how he was fighting one minute and drowning the next. And then he opened his eyes and looked up at the man who would surely kill him, and everything made sense.

HB surprised Boom by grinning slightly.

"Nigga, you got fucked up," he said drowsily.

Boom knew his bruises were visible. His nose was swollen, and he had at least one large contusion on the side of his head. But HB was worse for wear. He had a noticeable knot for each of the six blows Boom had landed. Plus he was bound with his arms behind his back. His legs were zip-tied to the chair.

Boom told him, "You ain't one to talk. Trust me, you look a lot worse."

His voice echoed in the mostly empty warehouse. The building was made of concrete and had no windows. The primary odors in the small space were mildew and dust, but the scent of the powerful men's musk and testosterone was quickly taking over.

"I almost had you," HB drawled. Sweat mixed with water glistened on his face and soaked his shirt. "I almost had yo ass. You had to kick me in the nuts."

"I know you ain't complaining about what went down in a street fight."

HB sighed. "Nah. I guess not."

"Why'd you do it?" Boom wanted to know.

HB looked him in the eyes. "'Cause you was gon' kill me."

"Why you think that?"

"'Cause we spent the whole day looking for your gal, and we couldn't find her. You wasn't finna let me live after that."

"I gave Mr. Brown my word that I wouldn't hurt you – as long as you didn't try nothing. He didn't tell you that?"

HB sighed again and nodded. "Yeah, he did. But I wasn't finna put my life in your hands just 'cause you made some promise. Only way to know for sure was to look out for myself."

Boom nodded. "I can respect that. Yo plan was to kill me?"

HB shook his head. "Naw. I was tryna knock yo ass out, so I could take yo car. Did you – you had a pistol on you, when you was searching me?"

"Yeah. Had it in my back."

"That's what I figured," HB said. "I was so busy tryna make sure you didn't reach for it, I let you catch me with that kick." He turned his head to the side and spat on the floor. "You wasn't gon' kill me, if we couldn't find her?"

Boom shook his head. "I gave my word."

HB watched his eyes. He took a deep breath and blew it out slowly. "But you is now…"

Boom nodded slowly.

"I guess you gon' fuck me up first," HB said.

"I don't have to. I respect you, and I don't want it to go that way. But it's up to you."

He stepped aside to reveal a small, metal table with an assortment of tools on top of it. He pushed the table forward, so HB could see what was in store for him. Boom had pliers, knives, a scalpel, salt, a large bottle of vegetable oil that was filled with hydrofluoric acid and the sledgehammer he'd taken to Perm's house a couple of days ago. He stepped away from the table and hefted a gas jug he had on the other side of the room. He placed it on the floor next to the table.

"It's still light outside," he told the lieutenant. "I don't care how long it take, and I don't care how messy it gets." He removed a pistol from the small of his back. "Or we can make it quick and easy." He placed the gun on the table next to his instruments of torment. "How you wanna play this?"

HB studied the items on the table and said, "You gon' torture me 'cause I don't know where yo girl at?"

"I don't know if you know where she at."

"I don't," HB said with a grimace. "You think I rode around all day looking for the bitch, if I knew where she was?"

Boom shrugged. "Maybe."

"*I don't know where she at*! You can do whatever you want, and you ain't gon' get no different answer from me."

"What about that uncle?" Boom asked. "You acted like you didn't wanna check on him."

"I didn't wanna check on him, 'cause I know he don't have shit to do with it."

"Why you so sure?"

"'*Cause he ain't in the game*! Peel said that nigga went to prison for some dumb shit, and he been a square since he got out. Peel tried to get him to hold some pistols once, and he wouldn't even do that. What lame you know gon' hold a bitch hostage? Sly tryna keep his nose clean. He ain't down with nothing illegal. That's why I made my move when I did. We was finna follow another dead end, and then I thought you was gon' kill me."

"What about Mr. Brown? Maybe he been knowing this whole time, and he sent me on a wild goose chase."

"He may have did that shit to you, but why the fuck would he put *my* life in danger over some bullshit? *We keep telling yo ass Peel was the only one who knew! If you would've asked him before you popped him, you'd prolly have yo bitch!*"

Boom was certain the man was telling the truth, which meant his chances of finding Asha were close to zero. If the men responsible for her abduction didn't know where she was, Boom had little hope of finding her on his own.

The anguish he felt at that moment was immeasurable, but he did not show weakness while in the presence of his enemy. His expression remained deadpan.

"Alright," he said. "I guess that just leaves your boss. I need to know where Mr. Brown lay his head."

HB's eyes widened slightly. His chest began to rise and fall with stuttering breaths. He said, "Killing Mr. Brown ain't gon' get yo bitch back."

"No," Boom conceded. "But it'll let the whole world know that if you fuck with me and mines, the wrath of hell is coming down on you. Don't matter how big you are or how many soldiers you got. Ain't nobody safe."

"And it'll let everybody know I'ma snitch," HB said.

"What a dead man care what people think of him?"

HB spat on the floor again. "You know better than that. A dead man's legacy is all he got left."

"So you willing to go through all this," Boom said, glancing down at the table, "for your *legacy*? Why you care what happen to Mr. Brown? He ain't yo people, right? Just some nigga you work with."

"You can save all this talk and do what you gotta do," Head Buster spat. "I don't give a fuck what happen. I ain't talking."

Boom sighed. He cracked his knuckles and stretched his arms, rolling his big shoulders to loosen them up. He slowly waved his hand over the table, making a show of deciding which tool he wanted to start with. He finally settled on the pliers. He picked them up and approached his target.

"You ever pulled somebody's toenails and fingernails off one by one?"

HB sneered at him, his breathing more ragged now.

"Shit hurt like hell," Boom told him. "Sometimes I can get a nigga to talk after only one foot."

"*Fuck you, Boom.*"

"Yeah. That's what they all say – before they start talking..."

He approached the chair and knelt to remove HB's shoes.

CHAPTER 48

WHEN HE ARRIVED at Mr. Brown's compound at two a.m., the moon was high in the sky, but it didn't provide enough illumination for the task at hand. Rather than scale the wrought iron fence encircling the mansion and attempt to locate the electric meters, as he'd done at OG Ruckus' house, Boom parked at the end of the block and climbed the electric pole.

Had a bystander seen him, they would've thought he was perfectly prepared for the job at hand, with his climbing belt, climbers and gauntlets. The only thing missing was a uniform that identified him as an employee of the electric company – and daylight, of course. No one would believe a technician was hard at work at this hour.

But Boom was banking on no one seeing him. It was too late for anyone to be walking their dog, and this upscale neighborhood didn't have residents hanging out at all hours of the night. Boom suspected the men guarding Mr. Brown were still awake, but that would play right into his hand.

Climbing the pole was a slow, tedious and dangerous process, especially at nighttime. Boom used the strap on his climbing belt to inch higher, one foot at a time. The climbers strapped to his legs had long spikes that extended past the bottom of his feet. Step by step, he pushed the spikes into the pole and then held the pole with one hand while moving the strap up.

Right foot, left foot.

Move the strap and lean back into it.

Right foot, left foot.

Move the strap and lean back into it.

His gauntlets were thick, leather gloves that protected him from splinters, all the way up his forearms. The man who sold him the equipment worked for the city's largest energy provider. He had to report his truck stolen to get away with the missing gear. The same man taught Boom how to pull the primary fuse on the transformer using a hot-stick. Boom hadn't been up on an electric pole in over a year. He hoped he could follow the wires well enough in the darkness to pull the correct fuse for the right house.

Three minutes later, he made it to the top. He checked the few lights that were on inside Mr. Brown's compound before he risked using the light from his phone to familiarize himself with the transformer. He took a deep breath and pulled the fuse. Sure enough, all the lights in the sprawling mansion went dark. Boom was halfway down the pole, moving a lot quicker now, when his phone vibrated in his pocket. He stopped for a second, so he could answer it on his Bluetooth.

"What up?" he asked in a hushed voice.

"That you, Boom, fucking with my lights?" Mr. Brown asked.

"Yup. 'Bout to be fucking with *you* in a minute."

"How you find me? HB gave you the address?"

"He didn't want to. It took hours, but he finally gave it up."

"You told me you wasn't gon' do nothing to him. You gave me yo word. That's the kind of nigga you is?"

"I told you I wouldn't do nothing to him if he didn't try nothing. He tried something."

"I'm supposed to believe that?"

"You ain't got to, but it's the truth. He a real soldier, though. You should be proud of him."

"Fuck 'em."

"That's cold," Boom replied.

"If he told you where I sleep, he ain't no real soldier. The hell wit' 'em."

When Boom made it to the ground, he hurriedly removed his equipment and stuffed it in an already bulky duffle bag. He then took off, almost fully sprinting.

"What you doing now?" the crime boss asked. "What's all that noise?"

"Tryna figure out how I'ma get in here," Boom said. "This a big ass house."

"How you know I'm even in there? Maybe ain't nobody in there."

"*Somebody* in there, or you wouldn't have known the lights were out."

"That don't mean *I'm* in there."

"I'm 'bout to find out..."

Boom had already cased Mr. Brown property, before he climbed the electric pole. He ran down a paved alleyway and hopped the fence into an adjacent neighbor's back yard. Using a chair he'd separated from the patio furniture, he quickly scaled the patio and made it to the roof of the house. It was impossible to stop the items in his duffle bag from clinking together, but Boom didn't think he'd been loud enough for any of the residents to hear.

They would definitely be alerted when he brought out the big kahuna, which was so rare, few people would know what they were looking at, even if they saw it in broad daylight. But Boom was saving that for last. In the meantime, he had a little light work to take care of. He unzipped his duffle bag and began to assemble his favorite weapon.

"You still there?" Mr. Brown asked.

"Yeah, but I gotta go," Boom told him, whispering now. He looked up at the house across from him and said, "Some of yo people out here looking for me. They gon' find me, if I keep talking to yo ass."

"Wait – it ain't gotta go like this. We can still work something out."

"I don't see how, unless you gon' tell me where Brionna at."

"You know I don't know."

"Yeah, you prolly don't."

"You ain't gon' get me," Mr. Brown said assuredly. "You know this motherfucker got a safe room."

"It still work with no power?"

"Bitch got a generator. Unless you got a nuclear bomb, I'm good."

Boom didn't doubt that. Most houses that size had a safe room that could protect residents from a fire or tornado. "Any women and kids in there?" he asked.

"I wouldn't insulate myself with no women and kids. I ain't no coward."

That was all Boom needed to know. He hung up on him and finished assembling his weapon. When he was done, he hefted the sniper rifle and eyed Mr. Brown's property through the infrared scope. There was one glowing figure in the back of the house and two more patrolling the sides, no doubt looking for the bearded menace. They were all armed with assault rifles.

Boom took out the one in the back with a chest shot.
THOOMP
The rifle's silencer muted his shot, but the target cried out before he began to choke on his own blood. The men on the sides of the house headed in his direction. Boom took aim at the one on the right, just as the back door opened. He adjusted his aim and hit the newcomer instead.
THOOMP
The man fell back into the darkness of the house. Boom returned his attention to the other two targets. Both were speaking in alarmed tones, trying to figure out where the shots were coming from. Boom caught the one on the left as he scurried towards patio furniture that wouldn't have shielded him if he had made it to it.
THOOMP
The man dropped and began to scream. Boom cursed himself for missing an instant kill shot. By the time he trained his next shot on the glowing figure on the right, the soldier was looking right at him but couldn't decipher one dark shadow from another. He stood staring for so long, Boom was able to line up a headshot.
THOOMP
He knew he only had a minute or so before any men remaining on the property figured things out and lit up the neighbor's house, so Boom didn't waste time breaking down

his rifle. He placed it on the roof next to him and unfastened the strap that secured the big kahuna.

The grenade launcher looked like a majestic revolver with a huge, multi-shot cylinder that could hold up to six projectiles. It was fully loaded. It cost an arm and a leg and was more illegal than any weapon Boom possessed. The doomsday survivalist he bought it from wouldn't say how he had acquired it or the ammunition. Boom hadn't asked too many questions. He only needed to know how it worked and *if* it worked.

He could think of no better time to find out.

He took aim and fired the first grenade through the back door.

BOOM!

The explosion was so ferocious, he couldn't help but stare at the destruction for a few seconds. No way did he need the next five shots.

Fuck it. In for an ounce, in for a pound.

He let loose with the rest of his shots, completely demolishing the back side and most likely the rest of the house as well.

He took a few moments to return the grenade launcher to his back. He kept the sniper rifle in hand as he hopped off the roof. Across the alley, Mr. Brown's compound was fully ablaze. The moment his feet hit the ground, Boom heard a sound behind him. He turned and came face to face with a Caucasian woman standing in her open patio door.

What the woman saw caused her baby blues to widen to almost comical levels: A dark figure wearing a ski mask, clad completely in black, a humongous rifle in hand, a duffle bag draped over his shoulder and a huge fire in the distance.

While Boom watched her, the woman slowly closed the patio door and turned her back on him with the same slow pace. She walked away, expecting to take a bullet in the back at any moment.

But Boom had already turned and scaled the fence again.

Thirty seconds later, he made it to his car unscathed.

PART SIX
DAY THREE

CHAPTER 49

THE NEXT MORNING, Boom sat in his living room watching a news report about the bloodbath at Mr. Brown's compound. He sat on the sofa, leaning forward with his forearms on his knees. The explosions were the biggest story on all of the local networks. So far, the police put the body count at six and indicated there were two survivors. Boom knew one of those survivors was the man of the house. Judging by overhead images of the destroyed mansion, it was unlikely anyone inside the home could've survived – unless they were bunkered inside a saferoom.

The detectives indicated there were no witnesses, which meant his targets had remained true to the code and refused to snitch, and the neighbor Boom encountered as he fled the scene had been too afraid to come forward with a description of the suspect.

By noon that day, as more details of the attack emerged, Overbrook Meadows' chief of police held a press conference. Boom had been following the developments throughout the day. Once again, he was glued to the screen when the top officer spoke:

"What happened last night was no accident. At least one assailant staged a coordinated attack from a location near the home. The suspect or *suspects* cut the power and shot four individuals with a high-powered rifle before setting off the explosions in the home. Detectives are still working to identify the nature of the explosions, but preliminary examinations lead us to believe they were caused by grenades."

That information set off a clamor among the pool of reporters.

One of them asked, "Is it true that the men who were killed were all armed?"

"Yes," the chief confirmed. "The victims on the outside of the house were armed at the time of their death. Judging by the location of their bodies, we believe they may have been trying to protect the property."

Another reporter said, "Sources have indicated the house in question belonged to Nathaniel Brown, who is believed to have criminal ties throughout the city. Do you believe this was an attempt to take Mr. Brown's life, and could you confirm he was inside the house at the time of the attack?"

The chief told him, "We are aware of ties Mr. Brown has to the mansion and to alleged criminal enterprises throughout the city, but he is not listed as the homeowner on the deed. At this time, we are not releasing any information on the survivors, but I can tell you that neither of them have been cooperative, as far as offering a motive for the attack or information on the suspects."

Another reporter said, "Some neighbors have reported hearing sounds before and during the explosions that makes them believe some sort of military weaponry was used. Have you been able to confirm this?"

"At this time," the chief said, "we have not determined the exact type of weapons that were used in the attack. If it turns out the explosions were indeed caused by grenades, it is likely they were deployed by a military weapon of some sort."

That revelation sent the reporters into an even bigger tizzy. They wanted to know what sort of person would have access to grenades and if the whole city was in danger.

The police chief ended the press conference by saying, "We do not believe the general public should be fearful of another attack. This incident was not random. The suspects targeted this location and the individuals at this location for a reason. We are aggressively working to the identify the assailants and their motive.

"The weapons used last night should not be in the hands of *any* citizen. Our investigators will work ceaselessly to get the men responsible for these grisly murders off the street as soon as possible. When we have more information, I will share it with you. Thank you for your time."

CHAPTER 50

BOOM SAT BACK on the couch and contemplated his next move. Retaliation from Mr. Brown was a certainty, and he also had to be wary of the police. He knew he'd have to get rid of the big kahuna. If he ever got caught with the grenade launcher, they'd give him the death penalty for sure.

But above all, it was Asha that consumed Boom's thoughts. No matter how many people he killed, he was no closer to getting his woman back. Destroying Mr. Brown's compound didn't make him feel any better about losing his partner, friend and lover.

He closed his eyes and racked his brain for the clue he was missing. Oftentimes when faced with a dilemma, the solution proved to be the most obvious.

What am I missing?

Boom felt he'd followed every lead, but there had to be something he hadn't looked into. His thought process was interrupted by one of his cellphones ringing. When he went to the bedroom to retrieve it, he was surprised to see Mr. Brown's number on the Caller ID. He'd never suspected the boss of being a rat, but with so much heat on him, the crime lord may have been forced to cooperate with the authorities.

Boom almost didn't answer, but there was a chance the boss was finally going to tell him where Asha was. He took a seat on the bed and accepted the call.

"The fuck you want?"

"You need to take some of that bass out yo voice and show me some respect," the kingpin said.

"Nigga why you calling me? I saw that shit on the news. How come yo ass ain't dead?"

"I told you you wasn't gon' get me."

"I don't know what you talking 'bout. You working for the police or something?"

"You know better than that."

"Nigga, I don't know what type of shit you on. If you got something to tell me, you need to hurry up and say it, 'cause you ain't finna get me talking on no wire."

"You really think I'm cooperating? That's disrespectful. I'm getting sick of you disrespecting me."

"*Say what you got to say!*"

"Alright. What I got to tell you is I know Brionna's name is *Asha*."

Boom was stunned that the boss had uncovered his woman's identity, but he didn't respond to it.

"You ain't the only one who got resources," Mr. Brown continued. "Just like you can find me, I can eventually find you. As far as Asha, it wasn't hard to find out who her people is. You finna get a call from somebody on facetime. You ain't gotta show yo face, but they got a little present for you, and you need to see it."

He disconnected.

Boom remained stiff and startled for a few seconds as he processed everything the man had said. He knew they hadn't found Tristan, and he couldn't think of who Mr. Brown was referring to.

When an unknown number tried to reach him on facetime, he went to the dresser and found a ski mask. He pulled it over his head before he took the call. The image that was revealed to him was not something that was foreign in his line of work, but the sight of four distressed victims turned his stomach. Boom had always avoided harming innocents. Whoever was on the other end of the line had the camera facing a small family; a woman, a man and two children. They were all on their knees with their hands raised high in the air. They were all crying and understandably terrified.

A man off camera ordered them to, "Say your names. You first, nigga."

"*Please don't hurt us!*" the father cried. "*I don't know what y'all want, but we didn't do nothing. Please leave us alone!*"

"*Nigga, say yo fucking name!*"

The man who was speaking stepped forward, but the camera angle didn't change, so Boom knew there were at least two assailants in the home. The man who spoke wore a bandana over half his face and had a ballcap low on his head. He had an assault rifle trained on the family.

"*I'm Richard!*" the father cried. "*Richard Turner! What do y'all want? We didn't do nothing!*"

"Say yo name, bitch," the masked man said to the mother.

"I'm Gloria Turner. This is my family. *We didn't do nothing wrong. Oh my God, please help us...*" She brought her hands together in prayer and was immediately rebuked.

"*Bitch, I said keep yo fucking hands up!*"

"*Mama,*" one of the children cried.

"*It's okay, baby. Just do what they say,*" she cried.

Boom's eyes widened as he watched. After what he'd done to HB, he knew he had no right to be critical of these tactics, but what he was seeing was appalling. The terror in the family's eyes, especially the children, filled him with rage and empathy as realization of who these people were dawned on him. The gunman proceeded to provide this information.

"Who Asha is to you?" he asked, pointing his weapon at the woman.

Her eyes widened before she said, "*That's my sister. What, why – what she got to do with this?*"

"She go by Brionna?" the masked man asked.

The woman was even more confused. She shook her head. "I don't, I don't know what you're talking about. I never heard nobody call her that. *What's happening?*"

The call abruptly went dead.

Boom shot to his feet. He had no idea how he'd find Asha's relatives or if he could save them in time, but doing nothing was not an option. It occurred to him that Tristan should know where Gloria lived. Boom hurried to the dresser to grab his primary phone, where he had Tristan's number. The moment he picked it up, his other phone rang. It was Mr. Brown again. Boom's heart raced as he answered.

"*Let them people go,*" he snarled. "They ain't got shit to do with this."

"Everythang's fair in war," was Mr. Brown's gruff reply. "I been telling you I wanted to end this, but yo ass wouldn't listen. Now you got them babies with a gun in they face. You ready to end it now, or I gotta tell my people to lay 'em all down?"

Boom no longer believed Mr. Brown was working with the police, and he understood that he'd been outplayed. Just because Mr. Brown didn't have a way to get to him personally didn't mean he couldn't find a roundabout. Boom knew Gloria had lost her youngest child a little over a year ago, and Asha loved her family dearly. Even if he never found his woman, Boom couldn't live with himself if he allowed Mr. Brown to murder her loved ones.

"*Stand down*," the crime lord said. "I should kill these motherfuckers anyway, for what you and yo bitch did to my men. But I know yo ass gon' keep coming back if I do. If you wanna dead this, we can. I'll call them niggas and tell 'em to let them people go. Or we can keep warring, and they'll be the next ones dead. What you wanna do?"

Boom was so enraged and disgusted, he could barely articulate his response. "Leave 'em alone," he finally said.

"That mean you done coming after me?"

Boom took a deep breath. When he blew it from his nose, the fumes were like steam. He said, "Yeah."

"You done coming after me and my people," Mr. Brown repeated. "Say it."

"I'm done coming after you and your people," Boom growled. "Just get yo men out them people house. And you gotta leave Tristan alone too."

"Now hold on, you know that nigga got it coming."

"If Brionna dead, and you gon' kill somebody in her family, you might as well kill 'em all, 'cause I'ma go hard on yo ass either way. If you want this to be done, you gotta leave 'em all alone."

After a pause, the boss said, "A'ight Boom. We'll dead it like that. This'll be the last time you ever hear from me. It better be the last time I hear from you."

Boom continued to fume.

"For the record," Mr. Brown said, "I'm sorry about yo gal. If I knew where she was, I'd go turn that ho loose myself. I wish I would'a never snatched the bitch. None of this shit was worth it." He disconnected.

It took Boom a full thirty minutes to get his emotions under control.

CHAPTER 51

HE LEFT AN hour later, headed for his safehouse on the west side. Tristan and Courtney were glad to be going home, but they both sensed a tragic shift in their protector. When they arrived at their apartments, Tristan remained in Boom's SUV, while Courtney took the kids upstairs.

He asked him, "Is everything alright? Did you find Asha?"

Boom shook his head slowly, without looking over at him.

Tristan grimaced. "What that mean, she, she dead?"

Boom looked him in the eyes then. He told him, "I don't know what that mean. It mean I didn't find her."

Tears filled Tristan's eyes and began to roll down his cheeks. He leaned forward and buried his face in his hands. *"This all my fault. I never should've called her. I never should've fucked with them niggas."*

Boom didn't say anything.

"You still looking for her?" Tristan asked him. "Is it something I can do to help?"

"Just get out the car," Boom said. "Mr. Brown and them ain't gon fuck with you no more."

"But I just wanna–"

"What you need to do is get out the car," Boom repeated. "I done went through a lot over yo shit. I don't wanna hurt you, but if you stay in this car another second..."

He squeezed his eyes closed and took a deep breath. He didn't open his eyes again until he heard the wannabe thug exit the vehicle and walk away.

CHAPTER 52

ON HER THIRD day of captivity, Asha's anxiety was at an all-time high. She could tell Sly was starting to feel the pressure too. He had become withdrawn, a lot less talkative than usual. Asha actually noticed the change the night before. When he brought her dinner, he seemed distracted and introspective.

"What's wrong with you?" she asked. "You get some bad news?"

"No," he had said, looking at her but not really *at* her. "It's nothing."

"You mad 'cause Peel's picking me up tomorrow?"

Hearing his nephew's name appeared to pain him, but he shook his head.

"No, I'm not mad about that. You wanna go home, don't you?"

"Yeah. I can't wait for y'all to take these damn chains off." When he didn't respond, she asked, "Do you know what time he's coming? Did he say it would be early in the day or..."

"He told me to keep you for a few days," Sly said, still not looking her in the eyes.

"Tomorrow's day three, so he might not come 'til nighttime, or in the morning the day after that."

Asha knew he was lying about something. "You telling me I gotta be here all day tomorrow?"

"Even if you do, it'll be your last day. It won't be that bad."

He didn't have an ominous tone when he said *last day*, but Asha wasn't comforted by his words.

On day three, he remained moody when delivering her breakfast and lunch.

At lunchtime she asked him, "Have you heard from Peel? Did he say when he was coming?"

"Yeah. I talked to him today. He said he'll be here tonight."

"*Really*?" Asha's eyes widened. She couldn't stop her heart from leaping, even though leaving with Peel didn't guarantee she'd be freed. For all she knew, he was coming to pick her up so he could take her to an alternate location and kill her.

"Do you know what's gonna happen after we leave?"

"He said he was gonna hand you over to your boyfriend."

Asha's eyes narrowed. The whole time she'd been there, Sly had never mentioned that he knew she had a man. She wondered how much he knew about Boom and what the bearded killer had been doing in the past few days to negotiate her release. She felt Sly wasn't being completely honest with her, but she believed that he'd been in contact with Peel. How else would he know about Boom?

"Did he tell you anything else?" she asked, "about my boyfriend?"

"He told me yo man's dangerous, and if he ever found out I was the one who was keeping you, he'd fuck me up for a long time before he killed me."

That definitely sounded like something Peel would say about Boom. But Asha didn't want Sly to think there would be repercussions if he let her go. In truth, she'd make it her life's mission to find and punish him to the fullest before he ended up in one of Boom's acid barrels. But she was stuck with him for the rest of the day, so she had to give him peace of mind.

"You ain't gotta worry about that," she said. "I'ma tell my boyfriend you treated me good, and you didn't really wanna do what Peel asked you. I'm definitely gon' tell him about yo cooking," she said and forced a smile. Her lunch that afternoon was lasagna. She could tell he pulled it from the freezer and had done nothing but bake it, but it was a lot better than a sandwich.

"You and you boyfriend ain't gon' try to find me, when y'all get back together?"

She shook her head. "Naw. I'll be ready to move on. Peel will be alright too, if him and my man worked out some kind of deal. I know my boyfriend mad about all this, but he don't never go back on his word."

Sly seemed to accept this.

By dinnertime his mood had changed again. Asha was disturbed to see that his inner demons had once again gained control of their human vessel. The shift was only in his eyes, but for her, it was so obvious, he might as well have sprouted horns and fangs.

He made a cheeseburger and fries for her that night. It was a simple meal, but he had put a lot of care into the preparation and presentation. He had toasted the buns and included all the fixings; lettuce, tomatoes and pickles. The fries were perfectly golden brown. Asha was so anxious, both about the monster that was feeding her and the possibility of going home, that she didn't have an appetite. She did her best to force the food down while he watched.

"Thanks," she told him. "This is good."

"People tell me I make good burgers. You think you gon' want another one? I cooked another patty, just in case."

Sly was back to his talkative self. And he was smiling now. Asha realized he was unaware that she saw something was different about him.

"You talked to Peel?" she asked. "He tell you what time he's getting here?"

"Yeah, he said he'll be here in a few hours."

"Really?"

"Yeah, you excited about going home?"

"Yeah, but after being here for so long, it's hard to believe it's finna be over."

"All good things must come to an end," he said whimsically.

"*Good things*? What was good about this?"

He told her, "I know this situation is fucked up, but I found a new friend."

Asha couldn't begin to explain how fucked up that comment was. Even if she could, she wasn't inclined to piss him off this late in the game. She reached for the drink he'd brought her and grimaced after taking a sip. Aside from the unexpected sting of the carbonated beverage, the soda had an aftertaste that didn't come from the Coca-Cola Company.

"What's this?"

"I brought you soda this time. I would've brought the juice I been giving you, but I think burgers taste better with soda..."

Asha had to battle every cell in her body to keep her expression neutral. Her thoughts were suddenly thrust 10 years back in time – to the murder that changed her life, long before she met Boom. While at a nightclub, she shot and killed a man who followed her to her car after slipping something in her drink. Asha would never forget the look in the man's eyes as he shadowed her at the club, waiting for her to succumb to his potion. She would never forget the look on his face when he opened her car door and was greeted with a pistol.

She didn't think about that night very often, but as Sly sat watching her, everything suddenly made sense. The understanding that she wasn't going home tonight, and this man planned to do ghastly things to her, almost made her throw up. Her whole body flushed with heat. She prayed perspiration wouldn't blossom on her forehead and reveal her inner turmoil.

She knew her life had been hanging in the balance from the moment she was abducted, but the next few minutes were the most critical. She could no longer rely on Boom or anyone else to rescue her from this deviant. She was on her own, and any missteps would cost her everything.

She tilted the cup again but didn't drink any before placing it next to her on the bench. She hoped Sly wasn't able to monitor the volume of the tainted soda from his vantage point.

"No, it's good," she told him. "I been wanting some soda."

His smile widened.

She reached for her burger and took another bite. She chewed heartily and then winced as she swallowed. "*Ouch, fuck!*" she exclaimed, grabbing her jaw.

Sly's eyes filled with concern. "What's wrong?"

"*My fucking cavity,*" she said, scowling. "This bitch always hurt when I get food stuck in it." She stuck a finger in her mouth, fingering the perfectly good molar. She then picked at it with her fingernail. "Can you get me a toothpick?" she asked. "The dentist said I got a exposed root. I don't know what that mean, but this shit hurt like hell."

Sly shot to his feet. "Yeah, I, uh, I think I got some." He turned and headed for the stairs and then stopped short. He turned back and eyed her food.

"I'm not gon' tear my plate up and use it to pick my locks while you gone," she promised. "You know I can't even pick a lock with no Styrofoam."

Sly hadn't given her a fork that night, so he thought it would be alright to leave her for a minute. He turned again and hurried up the stairs. The moment he was out of sight, Asha took the cup of soda and poured it in her sanitation bucket behind the bench. When she saw Sly coming back down the stairs, she turned the cup up and held it to her lips long enough to make him think she'd finished it. She licked her lips and placed the cup on the bench again. Even the scant amount of liquid on her lips tasted funny.

"You finished your soda?"

"Yeah, thanks. I was hoping I could use it to wash down whatever's stuck in my tooth, but it didn't work."

"Here," he said, tossing a toothpick over the line on the floor. It landed on her lap. "You want some more?" he asked as she pretended to dislodge the food from her tooth.

"What, food?" she said. "Naw, I'm full."

"No, soda… You want some more to drink?" Subtlety was not this creep's strong suit.

"I'm good. *Ooh.*" She winced again. "Got it." She pretended to roll a morsel around her tongue before swallowing it. "You want me to throw this back over there?" she asked, referring to the toothpick.

"You can put it on your plate and leave everything on the floor."

When she did, he said, "Go to the other side of–"

"Yeah, I know the drill."

She walked around the bench and stood on the safe side, while he retrieved her dishes. When she was done, she took a wobbly step as she returned to the front of the bench. She hoped the theatrics weren't too much, but from what she had tasted of the soda, he'd put enough GHB in it to knock out a horse. He shouldn't be surprised if it was already starting to take effect.

Sure enough his eyes widened. "You alright?"

"Yeah…" She placed a hand on the bench to steady herself. "I think I had too much to eat. Feeling a little dizzy."

He grinned. "I'm sure it's nothing."

Asha had always despised this man, but at that moment, she hated him more than the first day she got there. She was already shackled at the wrists and chained to the bench. Was that not enough of an advantage? He still felt the need to drug her to take the pussy?

"You should sit down," he suggested. "I'ma go call Peel and get an update on when he'll be here." He watched her for a moment longer before disappearing up the stairs.

Asha took a seat on the bench and blew out a sigh.

So far so good.

CHAPTER 53

WITHOUT A WATCH, it was hard to time it, but she remained in the same position for what felt like ten minutes before she lie on her back with both legs on the bench. She rolled her head so she could watch the stairway and then thought better of it. Her heart was beating so hard, she didn't think she'd be able to stop her eyelids from fluttering while she pretended to be unconscious.

Rolling her head *away* from the entrance was one of the hardest things she'd ever done. If he crept down there, she wouldn't see him coming or know what type of weapon he brought with him. Her soul thrashed like a caged tiger, but she willed her body to remain completely still. She waited and watched the wall and listened. She didn't hear anything, but that was no assurance.

If I open that door real quiet like, you wouldn't be able to hear it no way.

She strained her ears for the slightest sound. For all she knew, he was already there, standing over her, drooling, inching closer, inspecting to see if she was really asleep.

But he wasn't.

Forty minutes passed before she heard him descend the stairs again. Her heart froze. She listened to his footsteps as he drew nearer.

"Kiki, you alright?"

The closeness of his voice sent a tremor through her body.

"Hey, Kiki. You sleep?" He waited for a response and then said, "Peel's here. He's ready to take you to yo man. Wake up. Don't you wanna go home to your boyfriend?"

No response.

"*Kiki!*"

When he poked her, Asha nearly lost it. She was ready to spring into action. Thankfully the rational side of her brain held her back. Whatever he'd touched her with wasn't his hand. It was too hard and stiff. She imagined he was standing on his side of the line, poking her with the broom handle.

"*Kiki!*"

He nudged her again.

"Oh, you sleep ain't you?" His voice was softer now, in full creep mode. "What happened, baby? Had too much soda? You gon' be alright? You ain't dead, is you? I don't want you to die. I want you to feel *good*. I'ma make you feel real good."

When she felt his hand on her cheek, she remained limp and allowed him to roll her head towards him. In the split second it took for him to realize her eyes were open, she sprang to life with such explosive force, it felt like she'd been launched from a springboard.

Asha wasn't aware of the animalistic sound that came from her as she reached for him. It was somewhere between a scream and a growl. Sylvester yelped and squandered his advantage. He was bigger, stronger, and with Asha on her back, he had the positional advantage. But he tried to pull away, rather than mount an offensive. They struggled mightily, taking the battle from the bench to the floor. By the time Sylvester came to understand this was a life or death situation for him as well, the wild woman had him on the ground and clung to his back. She solidified the hold by wrapping her legs around his hips. The rapist knew exactly what was coming next.

He reached up, just as she tried to loop her arms over his head and get the cuffs on his neck. Her wrists made it past his forehead before he began pushing them in the opposite direction. She knew she hadn't reached his neck yet, but she yanked back with everything she had.

Sylvester screamed as the cuffs dug into his face, breaking his nose and two of his fingers.

"Aaaah!"

Asha yanked the cuffs down again and got below his chin this time. He still had a hand stuck between the cuffs and his Adam's apple, but it didn't matter. Asha continued to pull back. She released her scissor grip around his waist and brought a knee up to the small of his back. She pulled harder when his next scream was abruptly cut off and harder still when the cuffs dug into her wrists so hard, she thought she was being degloved. Sylvester clawed at her arms and hands with his free hand, but could not loosen her grip.

Asha cried and screamed and choked the bastard until his body had been limp for five minutes, and she knew with complete certainty that he could never harm her or anyone ever again. She finally released him and fell to a seated position next to the bench. She leaned back against it, her breathing labored, blood and sweat glistening on her face. She looked down at the monster and then kicked his shoulder, rolling him over to his back. His dead eyes bulged from his skull. They were almost completely crimson. She saw that she'd nearly cut his nose in half. The indention marks from the handcuffs were gruesome.

As she got her breathing under control and rubbed her sore wrists, it occurred to her that she may not have succeeded in freeing herself. Maybe all she'd accomplished was having a corpse down in the basement to keep her company. She crawled towards the body and checked his pockets. Relief washed over her when her fingers came in contact with a keychain.

Of course he brought the keys with him this time. This was going to be his big finale. The freak didn't want any restrictions.

Removing the handcuffs felt better than when she walked out of prison after seven long years. Two minutes later, she stepped out of the house and got a taste of fresh air for the first time in three days.

Until that moment, she never truly understood the meaning of the word euphoria.

CHAPTER 54

BOOM WAS ON the road, still questioning people who were even more wary of him after hearing what happened to Mr. Brown, when he received a call on his primary cell. He didn't recognize the number, which was odd, because he never gave this number to random associates. His eyes narrowed as he answered.

"Who dis?"

"Baby, it's me."

Boom nearly lost his shit. He stomped on the brakes in the middle of the street. The car behind him slammed its brakes too and barely avoided crashing into the back of his SUV. Boom didn't notice the driver blaring his horn.

"*Asha?*"

"Yeah, it's me."

Boom's eyes were wide. His mouth hung open. His whole body went numb.

"*What, what the, where are you?*"

"I'm on the south, on Irma."

"Baby, where you been? I been looking all over for you!"

"It's a long story. I can't talk right now. I'm using this guy's phone."

"Who? What guy?"

"Just some dude I flagged down."

"What address you at? I'm on my way." He got moving again. He looked over and saw that the driver he stopped in front of had pulled alongside him and was cursing him out. Boom rolled his window down and glared at him. *"You better get the fuck away from me!"*

The man's eyes widened. He slowed down and turned at the next corner.

"What's happening?" Asha asked him.

"Nothing. What's the address?"

"I'm on the side of the road, on Irma and Ash Crescent."

"Shit. I'm only five minutes away. You been over there this whole time?"

"Yeah."

"Baby, what the fuck. I been going crazy. I can't believe I'm talking to you right now."

"I gotta go," she told him. "This man want his phone back."

"Let me talk to him."

Asha handed the phone to the guy who had stopped to help her.

"What's up?" he said.

"My girl flagged you down?" Boom asked him.

"Yeah. I let her use my phone, but I gotta bounce. You need to take her to the hospital, dog. Her arms and shit... She got fucked up."

Boom felt his rage returning. "I need you to stay with her," he said. "Don't leave her alone. And let me stay on the phone with her. I'm five minutes away. I'ma look out for you when I get there."

"A'ight, man. I guess..."

A second later, Asha was back on the line. "Baby, I thought you was gon' come find me," she cried. "I didn't think I was ever going home."

"I'm sorry. *I tried so hard.* I don't know how many dollars I left on the table. None of it helped me find out where you was. Are you alright? That dude said you was messed up."

"It's just my wrists. I'll be alright."

Boom had so many questions, but he told her, "Don't say nothing else about it right now. I'ma couple of minutes away."

He gunned it on the next dark street. Asha could hear his engine screaming on her end of the line.

"Be careful," she told him. "I'm alright. You don't have to rush."

"Baby, if I have to drive this bitch through a house to get to you, that's what I'm gon' do."

CHAPTER 55

HE ARRIVED AT the intersection a few minutes later and gave the good Samaritan whatever he had in his pocket. The man's eyes widened.

"Dog, you ain't gotta gimme all this."

"Naw, it's cool," Boom told him, his eyes on his woman. Asha stood on the side of the road wearing the same outfit he'd last seen her in. He couldn't see any bruises in the darkness, but she was clearly distraught.

The man said something else, but Boom didn't hear him. He stepped around the car and wrapped his arms around the only thing that mattered. Asha broke down in his embrace. All the tension from the past three days came out in a flood of emotions. Boom held her so tightly, she knew she was finally safe. He would never let anyone else harm her.

Neither of them noticed the car drive away as they renewed their bond under the moonlight.

CHAPTER 56

WHEN THEY WERE in his truck, Boom turned the dome lights on and inspected her wounds. He seethed as he tenderly touched her wrists. He brushed the hair away from her face and was glad to see that none of the blood was hers. Asha told him everything she'd been through since crashing her bike. When she told him the name of the man who'd kept her and eventually met a violent end when he tried to rape her, Boom's mouth fell open.

"*Sly*?"

"Yeah," she said. "You know 'em?"

"Naw, but *goddamn*. I knew that nigga had something to do with this."

"What you mean?"

"I'll tell you about it later. Where this nigga at?"

"His house is up the street," she said and gestured in that direction.

Boom headed for Sylvester's home.

"He dead. We ain't gotta go back there," Asha said.

Boom didn't respond. His brow was furrowed. He looked meaner than a junkyard dog.

When they got to the house, Asha didn't want to go in.

Boom sensed her anxiety and told her, "You can wait in the car."

"No, I don't wanna be out here by myself," she said and opened her door. "I'll go with you."

Once inside, she took in more of the environment than she had when she made her escape. Sly's kitchen and living room were both neat. Without any womanly touches in the decorating, it was clear he'd been living a bachelor lifestyle. But his home wasn't cluttered with the usual mess of a man living alone.

Down in the basement, Boom took in the workbench his woman was chained to for three days and inspected the body on the floor. Asha was surprised when he suddenly kicked Sly in the face.

"*Motherfucker*!" he growled and commenced a full-on assault, kicking him again and again. He snatched the body off the ground and tossed it almost halfway across the room. He marched to it and began kicking again.

Asha moved to stop him, but she stopped short and backed away. In any normal situation, she would've felt this was a terrible way for Boom to get the anger out of his system. But she knew her man was not normal. She had to let him deal with this in his own way.

He tossed Sylvester's body again, this time against a wall and was finally satisfied when the brutalized corpse fell to a disgusting heap of twisted bones. The look in his eyes when he turned back to his woman was the most ferocious she'd even seen. His huge chest rose and fell as he caught his breath.

"I'ma go check the rest of the house," he told her.

Asha looked back at the workbench one last time before she followed him up the stairs.

Sylvester may have kept the common areas of his house in check, but his bedroom was where his demons had free range. They found a ton of pornography as well as sadomasochistic devices that he probably never used on willing participants. Asha shuddered as she stared at all the whips and chains. Some of the sex toys were so bizarre, she had no idea what they were used for.

Knowing she would've encountered some of this equipment, if she hadn't managed to defeat the rapist, filled her with the same rage her boyfriend felt.

Boom said, "Tell me again how much he suffered when you killed him."

"He was screaming like a bitch," she said, a deep scowl marring her soft features. "I got him in the face before I got the cuffs around his neck. Broke his nose. Fucked him up real good."

Boom nodded. "You know we gotta burn this bitch down."

Asha nodded. Of course they did. Boom would never leave their DNA at a crime scene that didn't get set ablaze.

CHAPTER 57

THEY WENT ALL the way to the north side of town to fill three gas jugs. Asha was still an apprentice, but she knew Boom traveled that far to make the police's job a little harder. The police were sure to check the cameras on any south side gas station if the clerk recalled someone putting gas in a jug, rather than in their car.

When they returned to the house, Asha remained in the SUV this time. Boom checked the house again and debated whether he should take a laptop he found in Sly's bedroom. It was sure to be filled with more porn, but there might be evidence of his atrocities, possibly involving other women. Boom decided he didn't need to know.

He took the laptop down to the basement, which was the only area of the house that wasn't carpeted. He used a sledgehammer to destroy it, making sure to smash the hard drive into oblivion. He then returned to the kitchen, where he left the gas jugs. He concentrated most of the gas in the basement but made sure to douse every room. He left a trail of gasoline from the front door, all the way to the driveway.

When he moved his truck to the street, Asha stopped him before he got out again.

She told him, "Wait. I wanna do it."

"Be careful," he warned. "It's gon' be a big one."

He wasn't wrong about that. Asha lit the fuse and watched a trail of fire quickly race towards the house. A moment later, the inferno was so powerful, it blew out one of the windows. Asha stood and watched for a moment, her hair billowing, her face glowing in the fire light.

When she got back in the car, Boom asked her, "You alright?"

"Yeah," she said with a nod. She closed her eyes and took a deep breath. "I can't tell you how good that felt."

CHAPTER 58

ON THE WAY home, Boom told her what he'd been up to in the past few days. Despite the depth of their relationship, Asha was surprised he'd single-handedly taken on Mr. Brown's army. What was not surprising was the number of people he'd bodied in the process. When her man set his mind to do something, a body count never mattered.

When Boom told her about the incident that put an end to his rampage, Asha stared at him with wide eyes that quickly filled with tears.

"*They hurt them?*" she asked. An image of her sister's family on their knees tortured her mind.

Boom shook his head. "Naw. They left 'em alone, but that don't mean they didn't hurt 'em psychologically. Innocents got a hard time dealing with shit like that. Them kids, I know they emotionally scarred. I'm sorry that happened to them."

Asha wiped the moisture from her eyes, but the tears seemed never-ending. "*This shit all my fault,*" she cried, "*everything that happened to you and them.*"

"Don't worry about me." He reached to hold her hand. "I don't regret nothing I did, even if none of it got you back. Mr. Brown had it coming. He been terrorizing this city for a long time. Ain't nobody ever put 'em in check."

"I gotta go see my sister," Asha told him.

"You wanna go now?"

She considered that and shook her head. "Naw, it's too late. Plus I look like shit. I ain't took a real bath since the last time I was home."

He took his attention off the road for a moment and looked her in the eyes. "You still beautiful."

Asha didn't know how that was the case, but she knew he didn't say it to make her feel better. He really meant it.

CHAPTER 59

WHEN THEY GOT home, Asha headed straight for the shower. Boom got in with her a few minutes later. He washed every inch of her body and then examined her wrists again. The handcuffs didn't break the skin when she threw them over Sly's neck and yanked back on them, but the bruises were deep. She knew they'd leave welts that would be visible for days, if not weeks.

"I think you should go to the hospital," Boom told her.

She shook her head. "I don't wanna go."

"But you could have nerve damage."

"I don't." She showed him she could wiggle all her fingers.

"Can you feel this?" he asked, running his fingers lightly across her hands.

She nodded. He repeated the process on her palms.

She told him, "I can feel that too."

"I still think you should go."

"I don't want to. I just wanna be here with you."

He sighed. "I hate that you went through all that by yourself. I know it took everything you had to get through it."

"Every night, all I could think about was getting home to you. That's what got me through."

His expression was pained as he leaned down and kissed her, more tenderly than he ever had.

When they got in bed, making love was the last thing on his mind. After all she'd been through, he thought she was too traumatized. But intimacy with her man was a huge part of her healing process. She needed him to make her feel normal again, and whole.

She stroked him, while sucking his bottom lip, and he rolled her to her back and slid in so smoothly and so fully, she knew that her nightmare had truly ended. She had reconnected with her soulmate.

That night, their lovemaking was smooth and sweet.

When she came, and told him, "I love you, Boom," her heart exploded when he told her, "I love you too."

She only thought she knew the meaning of the word euphoria. What she experienced earlier was nothing compared to this.

CHAPTER 60

THE NEXT MORNING, Asha went to visit her sister. When she turned onto Gloria's street, she wasn't surprised to see the family loading suitcases into their new Jeep, but the sight broke her heart. Asha's guilt felt like a boulder sitting on her chest. What happened next added a new level of heartache. When she pulled to a stop in front of the house, her niece and nephew headed to her car. Their mother said something, and they stopped in their tracks.

Gloria approached the children and turned them towards the house. She had to push the youngest one in that direction, when he didn't get moving quickly enough. Richard went to them and took their hands and led them away. Asha would never forget the look on her nephew's face as he continued to look back at her. And then her attention returned to Gloria, who was approaching her car. Asha started to get out, but her sister pushed the door closed.

"No, don't get out. You don't need to be here. I want you to go."

Asha couldn't hide the pain all of this was causing her. "Sis–"

"*What*?" Gloria snapped. She was as angry as any mother bear protecting her den, and rightly so. "What is it that you can possibly say that would make me feel better about what happened yesterday?"

Asha almost told her she was sorry, but she knew that was terribly inadequate.

"That's what I thought," her sister said. "I told you, Asha. *I told you.*" Gloria's eyes filled with tears, but her sorrow didn't override the anger and frustration. "I told you that man you're messing with was getting you into something bad. I didn't know how dangerous it was. I certainly didn't think your shit would end up in *my house*, but I told you. *I told you*! Do you have any idea what you've done to my family?"

Asha's face flushed with heat. Her fair skin turned two shades darker.

"I'm sorry, sis. But I took care of it. Y'all don't have to leave."

Gloria's eyes widened. "You took care of it? Really? Oh, well that makes me feel a helluva lot better! I guess we should all go on with our lives and eat breakfast and watch cartoons and act like nobody ever put a fucking gun in my children's faces!"

Asha's eyes filled with tears too. She grimaced as she shook her head.

"Was that you they called?" Gloria wanted to know.

Asha frowned in confusion.

"On facetime," her sister clarified. "While they were here, they called somebody, so they could see how scared we were. Was it you?" Tears ran down her cheeks.

Asha shook her head. She could barely look her sister in the eyes and face the devastation she'd caused her family.

"Then it was *him*," Gloria said. "Your *boyfriend*." She referred to Boom with such disdain, Asha knew she would hate him for the rest of her life. "He's the reason they did that to us?" Gloria's nostrils flared while she waited for a response.

Asha shook her head. "No, it's my fault. Everything happened because of me."

Gloria stared at her long and hard, as if she had no idea who her sister was. She noticed Asha's wrists then. Her chest shuddered when she saw the deep bruises.

"What the hell is happening to you, Asha? How much trouble are you in?"

"I'm not in trouble, G. I was, but everything is okay now."

"No," her sister said, shaking her head. "Not for us. I'll always love you, but…" She pursed her lips. "We don't want you around here no more. Don't ask me where we're going. Maybe one day in the future, if you turn your life around and leave that hoodlum you're messing with, maybe we can have some kind of relationship. But right now, I need you to leave me and my family alone. I'm sorry, but…" She broke down. She brought a hand to her face and tried to regain composure. "Just leave."

Asha knew there was nothing she could say to justify anything that had happened, so she didn't try. Boom always told her that if she adapted his lifestyle, there would come a time when she would have to cut ties with the people she cared about. If not, her enemies would find a way to use them against her. Asha had hoped he was exaggerating, but now she knew better.

She watched her sister return to the house, and then she slowly drove away.

CHAPTER 61

SHE HAD ONE last thing to take care of before heading home. She pulled into her cousin's apartment complex fifteen minutes later. Tristan's eyes brightened when he answered the door and saw her standing there.

"Oh, shit! Asha!"

He threw his arms around her and hugged her as tightly as Boom had the night before. Asha hugged him back. He backed away smiling. He took her hand and pulled her inside the apartment.

"Come in, girl! You gotta tell me what happened!"

In the living room, she was greeted by Courtney, her uncle Lucious and a man she didn't know. She assumed he was one of Tristan's running buddies. The atmosphere was a lot warmer than the cool reception she'd received at her sister's house. After exchanging pleasantries, Tristan asked her to follow him to one of the back rooms, presumably to discuss everything that had happened since she last spoke to him.

But Asha told him, "We gotta talk about that later. That ain't what I came here for."

"Oh," he said. "What's up?"

She said, "I told you I was gon' whoop yo ass the next time I saw you. We need to go down to the parking lot and handle our business."

Tristan's smile was frozen in place. "What? Girl, what you talking 'bout?"

Asha's expression was dead serious. "You know what I'm talking 'bout."

His smile fell. "You mad at me?"

"You know I'm mad at you, Tristan. But I don't hate you. I ain't gon' hate you when we done. But we need to take care of this. You ready?"

Tristan looked around anxiously. Uncle Lucius laughed.

"*Don't look over here, boy! She say y'all supposed to be fighting!*"

Tristan still couldn't believe it. "Asha, you trippin'." He looked to his woman for support. Courtney didn't let him down.

"Asha, you for real? You know he ain't gon' fight no woman."

"Yeah, he is," Asha said. "Or he just gon' stand there and get his ass beat. Either way, *one of us* gon' be fighting." Her attention returned to Tristan. "You ready? Let's go downstairs and get this over with."

Tristan thought his baby-mama's excuse was a valid one. "Asha, I ain't fightin' no female. I ain't got no reason to fight you."

"You ain't got no reason? You know damn well why I'm finna beat yo ass. Don't play dumb."

"I ain't fightin' no female."

SPLAK!

He didn't see the slap coming. The room went quiet as Tristan reached for his cheek, which was quickly reddening.

His father broke the silence with his hearty laughter. *"Goddamn, boy! She slapped the shit outta yo ass!"*

The other man in the room couldn't stop from cracking up.

Tristan's eyes narrowed. *"What the fuck you do that for?"* he yelled.

"Yeah, that's what I'm talkin' 'bout," Asha said, nodding. *"Use that anger.* Let's go." She headed for the door.

"I ain't fighting you, Asha!"

She spun on him and reached back, ready to deliver a vicious backhand. Tristan flinched and backed away from her.

"Stop, girl!"

Uncle Lucius shook his head. "Damn, boy. You can't let her do you like that in yo own house. If she want you to whoop her ass, go down there and whoop her ass. I know she family, but you got witnesses to say she asked for it. Gone and get this shit over with. Somebody hit you, you got a right to hit 'em back, even if it *is* a female."

"That's what you want?" Tristan asked her. "That's what you really want?"

Asha nodded. "Yes, Tristan. That's what I really want. You ready?"

With no other outs, he said, "Fuck it. Let's go."

He followed her downstairs into the parking lot. At that time of day, there were a dozen people in the area. They crowded around when they saw there was about to be a fight. None of the residents knew Asha, but they all seemed to know her cousin.

"Tristan, you finna fight a girl?" one of them asked.

"I don't want to! This what she want!"

"You bet not let that bitch kick yo ass," another person said. "You know we ain't gon' let you live that shit down."

They all laughed.

When she found a suitable spot, Asha turned and squared up. Tristan reluctantly stepped to her. He was nearly a foot taller and much heavier.

"You got my money?" Asha asked him.

"Huh?"

"You know what I'm talkin' 'bout, boy! I gave you five racks. Where my money?"

"I got some of it. I didn't know you wanted it back."

She shook her head. "Aw, hell yeah. You definitely need this work. Don't worry, we can still be cool when it's over."

"Huh?"

She jabbed him in the mouth. Like the slap upstairs, he didn't see it coming.

"*Oooh!*" someone exclaimed.

The crowd became animated and remained boisterous for the rest of the fight. Fighting a full-grown man was no easy task, especially for a woman her size. But what she gave up in brawn, Asha made up for with experience. Tristan had never been to prison. Asha spent seven years behind bars. Because of her attractiveness and slim figure, she had to defend herself from lesbians and other bad asses who thought she was easy prey, especially in the beginning. Few people in the free world knew how well she'd sharpened her fighting skills.

Tristan certainly didn't know.

After taking a couple of shots to the jaw, he gave up hope that this wasn't really happening and fought back in earnest. Asha dodged a couple of haymakers that would've wobbled her if they had landed and caught him with a three-piece combo; a right hook, left hook and then a hard jab to the nose. Tristan grabbed his honker, which immediately began to leak blood.

With a busted lip that was also bleeding and a couple of visible contusions, he backed away, saying, *"A'ight! That's it! I quit!"*

In that environment, it was uncommon for a street fight to end with one party simply quitting. Typically, the aggressor would continue to punch and stomp him into unconsciousness.

But Asha would never do that to her family.

"Bet," she said and lowered her hands. She turned and headed for her car. "I'll holler at you later. Take it easy, Unc. See you later, Courtney."

"Why you do my boy like that," Lucius said, laughing.

Courtney was too stunned to respond right away. She finally said, "Alright. Bye, Asha."

Listening to the chorus of jeers Tristan had to endure as she got into her car, Asha almost felt bad for him. She reminded herself that Tristan was the catalyst for the chain of events that sent armed men to her sister's house, and the pity went away.

As she drove home, she called her man and told him, "Hey, baby. I'm on my way."

"How'd it go with your sister?"

"She don't want nothing to do with me."

After a pause, Boom asked, "You gon' be alright?"

"Yeah, I guess so."

"Did you stop by your cousin's?"

"Yeah. I just left from over there."

"I told him you was gon' whoop his ass next time you saw him."

She chuckled. "You told him that?"

"Yeah. I wanted to do it, but that boy had me so hot, I would've fucked around and killed him."

"I took care of it," she said.

"You whooped his ass?"

"Yup."

He laughed. "Damn, I wish you would'a told me that's why you were going to see that nigga. I would'a met you over there, so I could see that shit."

"You might get a chance. It was a lot of people watching. I'm sure somebody gon' put it on World Star."

EPILOGUE

CHAPTER 62

THREE WEEKS LATER, peace had returned to the streets of Overbrook Meadows, even though the police were no closer to nabbing the suspect in the attack on Mr. Brown's compound. Due to the weapons involved, getting the killer off the street remained a top priority. As for Mr. Brown, he was back to running the city.

Asha and Boom took a little time off to let the heat die down, but on Saturday August 21st, they were ready to get back to work. They showered and then Asha returned to bed – not for her favorite activity with her man – but to perfect her aim for what was to be her most difficult kill yet.

She lie prone on the mattress with the weapon Boom selected for this job. The AR-15 was large and menacing. Asha was propped on her elbows, which allowed plenty of room for the clip that extended from the bottom of the rifle. Boom had affixed a green laser sight to the weapon. Unlike a red dot, the green sight could be used during the daytime. They calibrated it two days ago at a makeshift shooting range Boom built behind his trailer home in Alvarado.

Asha aimed the weapon at the bathroom door across the room. The door was approximately seven yards away. If they played their cards right, this would be the same distance between them and their intended target. Boom stood over her and checked out her form. Asha cocked the weapon and squeezed the trigger.

"*Pop*," she whispered.

"Make sure you keep the stock right on your shoulder," he told her. "You know it's gon' kick a little."

Asha did know that. At the shooting range, not only did the weapon kick when she fired a shot, but the barrel tended to rise up and a little to the left. Boom selected this semi-automatic weapon, rather than a fully auto, to minimize the recoil.

"What you aiming for?" he asked her.

That seemed obvious. He could see the green dot.

"Uh, the *door*..." she said sarcastically.

"Yo target ain't gon' be that big," he said. "Why don't you try aiming at the door*knob*."

Asha made the adjustment and held the sight on the new target.

"Put the gun down," Boom instructed, "and then pick it up and cock it and get back on the doorknob as fast as you can."

Asha followed his instructions as he counted.

"One... Two.... Three... Four– that's good," he said. "But you need to get it down to three seconds."

She tried again and completed the steps in three and a half seconds. She started over and was able to accomplish it in the time frame he requested.

He placed a foot on the mattress and said, "Put it down and try it again."

This time he began to rock the mattress. That took Asha back to four seconds, and she couldn't maintain the sight on the doorknob.

"Why you doing that?" she asked. "I ain't gon' be moving that much. Ain't like we gon' be on a dirt road."

"You gotta be prepared for anything. You don't know what it's gon' feel like."

"I know it's not gon' be as bad as this. And my target's head is bigger than that doorknob."

"What's wrong with being *over*prepared?"

"Nothing, I guess..."

He walked around the bed while she practiced again. He took hold of her ankles and lifted her legs.

"What you doing now?" she asked. "You gon' be messing with my feet while I'm taking the shot?"

"Maybe."

"You trippin'."

"I told you, you need to be prepared for anything."

"You taking it a little too far."

"Can you hold the shot or not?"

"Yeah, you see I got it."

Boom saw that the green dot was steady on the doorknob.

"Aim at the top hinge," he instructed.

Asha adjusted her aim to the top hinge of the door, while Boom did whatever the hell he was doing with her legs.

"The middle one," he said.

She lowered the sight.

Boom pulled her legs apart and said, "Door knob."

She adjusted her aim again and said, "I don't think this has anything to do with the job. You just like what you seeing back there."

"You the one doing this naked. You could've put some clothes on before you started practicing."

"You like it when I'm naked with a gun."

Staring between her legs, he couldn't deny that. "I do."

He crawled onto the bed and hiked her hips up.

"My ass ain't gon' be up in the air when I take the shot," she said with a chuckle.

"Can you hold your aim or not?"

"It's a little harder now, but you see I got it."

"This shit got me hard," he said.

She grinned. "I bet it do – *oooh!*"

He pushed the full length of his dick into her oasis without pretense or hesitation.

"*Aw, fuck...*" she moaned.

"What's up with yo shot?" he asked as he began to stroke deeply, but not too hard.

She focused on the sight and got the laser on the doorknob.

"Middle hinge," he said, pumping harder now.

His dick felt so good, Asha wanted to close her eyes and give in to the pleasure, but she followed his instructions.

"If you can hit all four while I'm fucking you," he said, "then I know for sure you ready." He slowed down and pushed in all the way. He then pumped his hips teasingly slow. "You like that?"

"*You know I do,*" she purred.

"I like what I'm seeing right now," he said, staring between his legs. "I love how you get wet for me. You ready?"

She took a shuddering breath. "*Ye, yeah.*"

"Put it down, and let's start over."

The moment she put the rifle down, he began pounding harder, digging for China with each stroke.

"Alright," he said. "Go."

Asha hefted the rifle and got it into position with the stock firmly against her shoulder. She cocked it and aimed at the doorknob. With Boom going so hard, the sight bounced around the target but never enough to be out of range for a headshot. She definitely maintained a tight enough aim for a shot to the chest.

"Bottom hinge," Boom said. His voice was calm, but the sex was anything but. Their thighs clapped as he stroked her so good, all she wanted to do was grip the sheets and scream his name.

When Boom saw that she was on target, he said, "Top hinge." When she maintained that shot, he said, "Middle hinge."

After holding that shot for a few seconds, she said, "*Uh, are, are we done?*"

"You can put the gun down, but we ain't done. I know you wanna ride this dick."

He backed out and lie on his back. Asha turned on the mattress and bit her lip when she saw his glistening piece. He was rock hard, naked just like her. She was torn between wanting to lick her juices off him and slurp down his offering or hopping on top as he suggested. She decided it was okay to be a little selfish. She crawled over him and shuddered as she eased down on his pole.

This dick...

Today was all about her. This was her job, and it was a big one.

CHAPTER 63

THREE HOURS LATER, they were on the freeway, traveling a little over the speed limit, headed north on I-35. Their target was three cars ahead of them in the middle lane, in a black-on-black Lincoln Navigator. Boom drove a Suburban. He would've preferred a speedier ride, but the spacious SUV was better suited for the task at hand.

His disguise featured a goatee with a high-top hairstyle and dark shades. Asha didn't have a disguise, but her hair was pulled back. She had a ski mask waiting for her. She didn't need it until she was in position.

Boom was focused and quiet as he drove. He hadn't spoken at all since they began tailing the target.

He didn't look her way when he asked, "Alright. You ready?"

Asha took a deep breath and nodded. "Yeah. I'm ready."

She reclined her seat all the way back and then turned and crawled between the driver and passenger seats, making her way to the back of the truck. She remained low, on her elbows and knees, her head never rising above the passenger windows. All the seats in the back of the truck had been folded forward, allowing for maximum cargo space. Asha had so much room back there, they might as well have been in a van.

Her equipment was waiting in the back of the truck. She pulled on the ski mask and then hefted the AR-15, exactly as she had done in their bed. The only difference now was the surface she rested her elbows on was a lot harder than the mattress, and this was not a drill. Her heart began to drum at a quickened pace, as it always did when she was about to make a kill.

Due to the length of the rifle, Asha's feet extended between the two front seats. She had to be careful not to kick the gearshift while Boom was driving. When she was comfortable, she cocked the weapon, chambering a live round. She took a deep breath and told her man, "Okay, I'm in position."

"Who you gon' hit first?" he quizzed her before he left the lane he was traveling in.

She said, "The target."

"Why not the driver?"

"Because he's not a threat, and the target is my objective. If I hit the driver first, the car might swerve out of my line of sight, and I won't get the target."

"Who you gon' hit after that?"

"The front passenger – unless he's the target, and I already got him."

"Why the front passenger?"

"Because he's the biggest threat, once I start shooting."

"Who you getting after that?"

"Anyone else in the car, and I'll save the driver for last."

"Why you saving the driver for last?"

"Because I don't want him to swerve before I'm done."

"He might try to ram into us when you start shooting. If he does, you'll probably fall out the truck and get ran over."

"I have to take that risk."

Satisfied with her answers, Boom moved from the right to the middle lane. Now he was behind the target, three cars back. He transitioned again to the left lane and sped up.

Asha's heart froze when he told her, "I'm passing him now." A moment later he said, "The car in front of him ain't giving me too much room. I gotta cut the Navi off to get in front. You know what that mean...?"

"The driver prolly gon' suspect something, so I gotta be fast."

"Don't wait for the hatch to go all the way up," he said. "Soon as you see the target, take the shot."

"I got it. I'm ready."

"Alright. Here we go."

Asha felt the truck jerk to the right as Boom got in front of the Navigator. Two days ago, he disabled a safety feature on the Suburban that wouldn't allow the hatchback to open while the car was moving. With the push of a button, Asha suddenly saw daylight and then the freeway and finally the front windshield of the Navigator. She was already staring down the sight of her rifle. Her laser sight had daytime visibility up to 100 yards. She only needed a fraction of that.

She quickly checked the passenger. When she saw he wasn't the target, she moved her aim to the man in the backseat. She didn't notice the look on the driver and passenger's faces when they saw the hatchback go up and realized they were under attack.

Before the driver could react, Asha locked eyes with the man in the backseat. Mr. Brown didn't have time to blink before she squeezed the trigger.

BRRAATT!

Through the sight, she watched his face explode. The exit wound was so big, the backside of his skull and a good deal of his brain was propelled through the shattered rear windshield.

There was no one else in the back, so Asha returned her attention to the front seats. She hit the passenger next. By then he was reaching for something.

BRRAATT! BRRAATTT!

The next thing he reached for were the new holes in his chest and neck. Blood splattered the cracked front windshield.

By then, the driver had taken a defensive maneuver, but Asha's driver outmaneuvered him. Boom jerked his wheel to the right and remained in front of the Navigator when it switched lanes. Asha lined up her shot in two seconds and hit the driver in the chin and chest.

BRRAATT! BRRAATT!

The car swerved violently to the left and sideswiped a Camry.

"Got 'em," Asha told her man. *"Let's go!"*

Boom lowered the hatchback as he gunned it towards the 18th Street exit, headed for his north side safehouse.

Once there, they planned to ditch the Suburban and take off in his Charger.

One minute after the last gunshot, Asha was back in the passenger seat, her eyes wide, her chest rising and falling. She took a deep breath and blew it out slowly. Boom looked over at her.

"You sure Mr. Brown dead."

"Yeah," she breathed. "No doubt. Hit 'em in the face."

"You got everybody else in the car?"

"Yeah. I'm positive."

His eyes returned to the road. "You sure that was a good move, killing that nigga?"

Asha frowned as she stared at him. "*What*? Are you serious? You asking me that *now*?"

"I'm just asking."

"A little late for that. If you didn't want me to do it, you could'a told me weeks ago."

"I just wanna make sure you did it for the right reasons, and you okay with the possible repercussions."

"I did it 'cause he sent goons to my sister's house and locked me up with that pervert. That ain't a good reason?"

"It is. I ain't mad at you." Ten miles down the road, he took the 18th Street exit and merged with the traffic on the service road. There were no cars speeding towards them in the rearview mirror.

He said, "But I did give my word that I was gon' leave that man alone."

"You did leave 'em alone," Asha countered. "*I'm* the one who killed him."

"I'm sure most people would put an asterisk on that, seeing as how I'm the driver and chief strategist."

"*Chief strategist...*" she said with a grin. "I guess I should be asking if *you* okay with people thinking you went back on your word?"

He shrugged. "They ain't gon' be able to prove I did it. I'm sure the police will think it's the same person who blew his house up. But they can't find that nigga. Last I heard, that dude done ran all the way to South America."

Asha chuckled nervously and then said, "South America don't sound half bad."

"We might have to go to war," Boom said, "before we can think about retiring."

"You think somebody on Mr. Brown's side gon' come after us?"

"Maybe."

"You been to war with them before – and you won."

"I wouldn't say I won. It was more of a stalemate."

"Well, you killed more than a dozen of them, and they killed *zero* of you."

He smiled.

"And you didn't even have yo top soldier with you," Asha continued. "They definitely don't stand a chance against the two of us."

Boom looked over at her. "Yeah, you prolly right. I'll tell you this, tho': If we *do* go to war, we gon' make sure we get some paper off every one of 'em we peel. No sense in leaving the money with the bodies. We'll probably have our five mil', when it's all said and done."

Asha knew what that magic number meant. "And then we can retire..." she said, her smile wide, her eyes twinkling.

"Yeah," Boom said. "I don't know about South America, tho'. Nigga should be able to find somewhere right here in America to settle down and start over. Maybe have some kids…”

Asha's heart fluttered. "You want a little Boom-Boom running around the house?"

Boom laughed. "Yeah, what you think about that?"

"*I think we need to start killing these niggas right now*! Hurry up and get this shit over with!"

Boom looked at her sideways. "What the fuck I done created?"

"You know exactly what you created. And you love every bit of it…"

KEITH THOMAS WALKER

ABOUT THE AUTHOR

Keith Thomas Walker, known as the Master of Romantic Suspense and Urban Fiction, is the author of more than two dozen novels, including *Fixin' Tyrone, Life After, The Realest Ever,* the *Backslide* series, the *Brick House* series and the *Finley High* series. Keith's books transcend all genres. He has published romance, urban fiction, mystery/thriller, teen/young adult, Christian, poetry and erotica. Originally from Fort Worth, he is a graduate of Texas Wesleyan University. Keith has won numerous awards in the categories of "Best Male Author," "Best Romance," "Best Urban Fiction," "Best Young Adult Romance," "Best Duo," "Book of the Year," and "Author of the Year," from several book clubs and organizations. Visit him at www.keiththomaswalker.com.